THE SHADOW OF THE OBJECT

ALSO BY CHLOE ARIDJIS

Book of Clouds
Asunder
Sea Monsters
Dialogue with a Somnambulist: Stories,
Essays, and a Portrait Gallery

The Shadow of the Object

CHLOE ARIDJIS

Chatto & Windus
LONDON

1 3 5 7 9 10 8 6 4 2

Chatto & Windus, an imprint of Vintage, is part of the
Penguin Random House group of companies

Vintage, Penguin Random House UK, One Embassy
Gardens, 8 Viaduct Gardens, London SW11 7BW

penguin.co.uk/vintage
global.penguinrandomhouse.com

First published by Chatto & Windus in 2026

Copyright © Chloe Aridjis, 2026

The moral right of the author has been asserted

Penguin Random House values and supports copyright. Copyright fuels creativity, encourages diverse voices, promotes freedom of expression and supports a vibrant culture. Thank you for purchasing an authorised edition of this book and for respecting intellectual property laws by not reproducing, scanning or distributing any part of it by any means without permission. You are supporting authors and enabling Penguin Random House to continue to publish books for everyone. No part of this book may be used or reproduced in any manner for the purpose of training artificial intelligence technologies or systems. In accordance with Article 4(3) of the DSM Directive 2019/790, Penguin Random House expressly reserves this work from the text and data mining exception.

Set in 12.7/15.2pt Bembo Book MT Pro
Typeset by Six Red Marbles UK, Thetford, Norfolk

Printed and bound in Great Britain by Clays Ltd, Elcograf S.p.A.

The authorised representative in the EEA is Penguin Random House
Ireland, Morrison Chambers, 32 Nassau Street, Dublin D02 YH68

A CIP catalogue record for this book is available from the British Library

HB ISBN 9781784746377
TPB ISBN 9781784746384

Penguin Random House is committed to a sustainable future
for our business, our readers and our planet. This book is made
from Forest Stewardship Council® certified paper.

For if 'tis Tangible, and hath a Place,
'Tis Body; if Intangible, 'tis Space.

LUCRETIUS, *De rerum natura*

I

The fewer the props the greater the magic, a famous magician once said, although in my case it wasn't the flourish of a wand but the wave of my own hand. My own hand made certain things vanish and conjured others into existence. Yes, its mere movement brought about more change, more transformation, than any magic trick. On night three of my visit home, after watching a film with my parents in their bedroom, I'd risen from my chair and waved goodnight. The mistake, we later concluded, had been to wave. All the dog saw, we concluded, had been a disembodied hand.

A hand – floating, beckoning, threatening – mid-air.

He had watched over our home for eleven years, this dog, been taken for daily walks and given the run of the garden, slept pressed against my parents' door each night, a magnificent Alsatian with a coal-black face and golden eyebrows, occasionally he growled but for the most part he remained composed, his inner life and ours mysteriously, harmoniously, aligned. Until that moment when he was possessed by an unknown force, his eyes glowing amber, teeth sinking into my hand.

One second a searing pain, the next nothing, the pain too new, too vast, to identify. My mother threw the television control and missed. My stepfather reached for the cane by his bed, until then never used on anyone, and after receiving a blow on his hind legs, there was no choice, the dog released me, but not without difficulty since one of his canines snagged on a bone and had to unhook at just the right angle.

At night he turns wolf, my mother would say, and it was true his mood grew feral after dusk. But until then, the wolf had protected us.

The elderly taxi driver who took us to the hospital seemed lost in thought as he wound through the sinister scrublands of Chapultepec Park. Please hurry, it's an emergency, we urged, but the man took a meandering route via the *tercera sección*, deserted apart from the packs of hounds that were the spirit of its wilderness and ravines.

We arrived at the hospital after thirty minutes, or perhaps it was forty or forty-five, time marked only by increments of pain, followed by limbo in a waiting room inhabited by a silenced television and a howling boy. Old episodes of *El Chapulín Colorado* played across the screen, the sight of a grown man dressed as a red grasshopper even more absurd on mute, my stepfather kept laughing and my mother now and then too, how could they laugh when I had just been bitten by our dog, well, how could they laugh full stop, and as the pain shot up my arm I wondered how much more I could endure.

The clock on the wall read 2:25 when the hand surgeon arrived, bathed and perfumed, in a black leather jacket. I followed the man to a cubicle, where he drew the curtain, and in that snug space he unwrapped the provisional bandage my mother had thrown on and poured alcohol and iodine into my wounds, my hand on fire as he set to work removing some of the debris. Eight deep bites, he counted, on the front and the back and in the fold of my thumb, but I couldn't bring myself to look.

From that moment to the hospital bed, only a few memories survive:

The surgeon speaking into the phone as he booked the operating room for dawn, his delivery as straight as a hospital corridor, a professional urgency that didn't allow for nuance or digression. I attempted, unsuccessfully, to read my fate in his words.

The anaesthetist's customary question – Vodka, rum or tequila? – before administering the jab.

Tejido necrótico. The first words heard upon waking. Not a punk rock band, not necromancy or necropolis, but necrosis. Local dead tissue, a necrotic citadel, a small cemetery of cells, in my hand.

Square room, low ceiling.

Remedies descending in a drip, bed fitted with contraptions.

A greyish light at the windows.

Anaesthesia on the ebb: edges and angles acquiring definition.

Fastened to the corner of the ceiling, an enormous television.

Fastened to the wall by the door, a pump with disinfectant gel.

And, pasted onto the scene like a collage, my mother and stepfather.

How long had they been there, side by side on the sofa?

I hadn't visited home in three years and now, here we were.

How is Diogenes? I asked. The voice that emerged from my chest was hoarse and peculiar and I had to repeat my question.

His name was Diogenes. Diego for short. Two or three syllables suit a dog much better than four, and from puppyhood onwards we used his full name in conversation but Diego when addressing him, not an exact diminutive of Diogenes but he didn't seem to mind. And anyway, as he grew older he often wouldn't respond when called, he'd lift his head and then drop it back down, the gravity of the years stronger than any impulse towards obedience or curiosity.

Diogenes was sulking and ashamed and keeping to the corners of the house, my mother said. Aware he'd done something wrong, uncertain what.

Put him down, a chorus had begun, put him down. Our neighbours were insisting, and a few relatives too. You will never feel safe again with him in your midst. But no, how could we? He was part of the family. Ignore the chorus, we agreed. Our only action would be to follow the veterinarian's advice and neuter him, in case an excess of testosterone was to blame.

The issue had been laid to rest, the dog would be snipped and the story would end there, when the surgeon entered the room. The door was open but he knocked to announce his presence, then helped himself to some gel and rubbed his hands together as he approached. This time he was accompanied by another man. Bald, pockmarked, with glasses. The *infectólogo*. Grave-faced, they explained they couldn't seal my hand just yet, there was still too much splintered bone inside, and therefore too much risk of infection. And with the risk of infection, they wielded a new word. Osteomyelitis. I would need at least one more surgery, possibly two, and for the time being should remain in hospital. The antibiotics I was receiving were too strong to take orally and had to enter through a drip, and my hand should remain protected from the dangers of the outside world.

The outside world. Everything familiar belonged there, not here.

As they spoke, each man reiterating what his colleague had said, I saw the remaining days of my visit home spiralling down the drain. Old friends whose numbers I wouldn't be dialling. Neighbourhoods I'd have to wait another couple of years to wander. Fewer hours conversing with the past in charged spaces of the house. Not to mention ten months saving for the plane ticket. All because of Diogenes, a dog that'd been fed three times a day every day of his life, wet food and dry food and water, along with countless treats and vitamins and supplements to keep his joints in action. How little had been expected of him in return, apart from to be a good dog and defend the house from intruders. And in this case the intruder had been my hand, at least that's what we had to conclude since any other explanation would have been too unthinkable. Night blindness and cataracts, is what the vet later said, adding that Alsatians grew skittish with age. His words corroborated my mother's theory: the dog had seen nothing but a disembodied hand.

A hand out of context, unattached to a body, was indeed an unsettling sight. A hand gone rogue, no longer following orders from headquarters. I'd seen a few myself, and every now and then one crept back into memory, particularly the spirit rapping hand in an exhibition about the occult, a life-sized model of a female hand with a lace cuff and manicured nails. It sat very still yet I could feel the tension, fingers alert for any message coming its way, poised to reply with one rap for 'yes', two for 'no', and three for 'doubtful or unknown'. Nearly as macabre was the wax hand of a saint in a reliquary in a Mexican church, the nails painted blood red, a thick gemstone on the ring finger. An individual, parcelled out. So much intention is loaded into one lone hand, inevitably more perturbing than two, and if Diogenes saw a disembodied hand that night in the sanctuary of my parents' bedroom I couldn't blame him for leaping to conclusions.

My visitors were restless. Repetitive motions gave them away. My stepfather flipped through the pages of a magazine, even from a distance I could see he wasn't pausing for more than adverts and headlines, while my mother kept stepping out to scan the corridor as if awaiting some mysterious annunciation. I had flown over to see them yet the ocean remained between us. At six o'clock they rose to leave; it was time for dinner. Before departing my stepfather went over to the television and switched it on, flicking through the channels until coming upon the antics of the Chapulín Colorado once again, and I couldn't help wondering whether this character roamed the entrails of the hospital, waiting to resurface through whatever portal he was granted.

I bade the nurse who came in shortly afterwards to turn it off, and as she readied the thermometer I asked her to tell me what exactly held this television looming dangerously over my bed in place. It's fastened to the ceiling with massive screws, she said, and then, as if reading my mind, added, During our recent earthquake many things went rolling off and some patients were even severed from their drips but the televisions stayed put, she explained, as she held the thermometer up to the light (no fever) and rearranged the pillows into a snowy stack.

The next afternoon my mother came by on her own. After setting down a tote bag overflowing with snacks – my stepfather worked for Sabritas – she took a seat on the sofa and sighed. What to say, she said, I hope your hand mends quickly. Today her face was a map of worry and I knew what she was thinking. Whenever something went wrong in life, though never anything as dramatic as this, we would think about how different it would be if my father were still here. He'd been gone for many years, vanished one Sunday into the labyrinth of the city, after going to play chess with a colleague. At first we thought something catastrophic had happened, perhaps he'd been struck by a bullet intended for someone else, but the truth was delivered three days later in the form of a letter: my father had left us. He would, it seemed, never be back. Too young to fully accept this fact, for years I convinced myself that the man who was my father had been dispatched in a game of chess, that he'd become a pawn and been captured by his opponent, and the person who'd posted that letter was his double. Not entirely off the mark, I later discovered, since through cousins it was revealed he had another family up north, and had been leading a double life. Everything he'd established with us – rituals, confidences, intimacies – had its replica elsewhere. Nothing had been unique, nothing sacred. My mother didn't mention him, I didn't mention him, but there he sat in the room with us.

★

The light seemed concentrated in their faces, the shadow in their buns. That night the nurses lowered the dose of painkillers and my stupor was replaced by a blissful headiness that skirted sleep, abandoning me on the same shore each time. My body clock was completely askew – I had flown from London to Mexico only a few days before and shortly afterwards landed in hospital, where the passage of hours acquired an even stranger aspect and my irregular patterns of sleep produced a bizarre quality of thought. Every now and then a sharp pain pierced my hand and ran up my arm, testing the network of communication. My desire for a sleeping pill grew and grew, anything would do, zolpidem or zopiclone or temazepam, but when I asked the nurse she shook her head. Controlled substances must be approved by the doctor on duty and said doctor was in the midst of an emergency. Not even half a pill? I hadn't experienced such a craving in a while; usually, either I had my pills at hand and took one straight away or else I didn't have any anywhere, in which case I wouldn't allow the thought to possess me.

I listened to sounds distanced from their sources, seconds pooling into minutes, minutes into the purrs of machines, purring in a different language from my machine at work, and now and again these machines would merge with the sound of elevator doors stuttering open and closed, until into this mechanical soundscape entered the voice of a woman, an elderly woman, calling out for a nurse, a doctor, anyone. Her pleas grew louder, more desperate, her voice cracking in despair, could no one hear her but me, I wondered, as I slipped out of bed and started down the corridor with my drip.

A few metres away a group of nurses huddled round a magazine. One of them looked up and asked what I needed, why I was up and about. The rest of the nurses reluctantly tore their eyes away from the page. A woman is calling out, I said, she sounds old and forlorn. Yes, we are aware of her, but she wants water and isn't allowed any fluids until tomorrow, they said, then asked whether there was anything further before refusing my second request for a pill.

Disappointed with the expedition and in no hurry to return to bed, I chose a more circuitous route to my room. Instead of heading back in the direction I'd come from I turned here and there at random. The corridors wrapped around an inner court, you could peer down three floors and into the lobby with its striped sofas and raucous gift shop, a jamboree of colour before the mood turned clinical. To my left ran a sequence of open doors exuding a bluish tint and I hurried past, more fearful of an infectious emptiness than of disrupting the sleep of any patient, and then took the first right, my drip nearly catching on the corner, and it was then that I saw her, a strange figure in a wheelchair, a hybrid of woman and chair, her gaze burning a path down the corridor, one moment flaring towards me and the next completely still, yes, that was my first impression of her, an intriguing silhouette at the end of the corridor. There may have been a blanket thrown over her shoulders, I no longer recall. Her hair may have been loose or pinned up. At that moment she wasn't operating any of her illusions, she was separated from her milieu, no dissolving views no spinning no slits no slats no pages of books read backwards to reveal a hidden design, indeed no hidden design, simply a figure in the darkness projecting her gaze, nothing but a gaze, yet that gaze had the steady force of a beam of light. I turned around, unnerved, and hurried back to my room and again rang for the nurse, who called the doctor. Now freed from his emergency, he handed me a glass of water and a zopiclone.

Sometimes an animal leaves its mark on you for life.

When it comes to dog breeds and the force of their bites, Alsatians come after mastiffs and Rottweilers. Breeds such as pit bulls are more tenacious, that's what makes encounters with them so gruesome, but the Alsatian's bite is actually more powerful, with a 238-measure bite force in its jaws, calculated in pounds per square inch . . . Let me put it into context, lions have a 650 bite force, jaguars 1,500. A polar bear's is 1,200, a gorilla's 1,300, a hippo's 1,800 . . . As for the Nile crocodile, its bite force is around 5,000 . . .

That's enough, my mother interrupted, aware the hand surgeon was getting carried away.

I'm just saying why your daughter must remain here for a while longer . . . We can't take any chances.

The only chances being taken were with my sanity, I should have said, although I would've found it hard to explain exactly why, especially since part of me was starting to enjoy this hospital stay. After all, hospital stays offer a rare occasion to check out – during the rest of life you are checked in and accountable, but as a patient you are absolved of most responsibility, nothing expected of you except to mend. On the contrary, you can make demands on others, even extravagant demands every now and then, and thanks to my travel insurance I was at the fanciest hospital in Mexico City, in my own room with an adjustable bed and people waiting on me night and day, a situation I had never found myself in before. The outside world may forget about you while you're in hospital but to be forgotten, temporarily, isn't such a bad thing.

On my stroll that evening I avoided the nurses' station and took a left down a stretch of corridor with a hissing light, our wing more desolate than ever as though the other patients slept more deeply, more medicated, even further removed from our suspended present, apart from one face that appeared briefly at a door, wide-eyed and ashen; uncertain whether it was man, woman or spectre, I quickly hurried on. Such a stark sense of corridor desolation hadn't hit me since adolescence, on one of the first occasions I'd spent hours at a hospital, not as a patient but as a visitor, and not as a visitor paying her respects, but as a reveller.

The rave had been held in a huge building in Mexico City, soon to be the first AIDS hospital in Latin America. Shortly afterwards, beds would be delivered and the space transformed into a place of intensive care, but before that a charity had decided to raise money for incoming patients. The promoters had papered bars, clubs and record shops with flyers, and by eleven the party had reached full capacity and the bouncers began turning people away at the door. Wild and reckless we ran through the strobe-lit rooms, each one powered by a different DJ and his or her techno anthems, and at moments it felt like heresy to be dancing and cavorting in a space that would soon be marked by suffering but I convinced myself we were infusing the place with life, with a life force to be administered to future patients in doses small enough to guarantee there was enough for everyone, and with that idea in mind I was able to plunge freely into the night.

The only conversation I remember having was with a young European, possibly Belgian, wearing LED gloves that glowed at the tips, and after I'd paid him a compliment he mentioned he'd worn them recently to a rave near Zurich, one of the best parties he'd ever been to, he said, except that at around four in the morning the DJ had suddenly stopped the music and asked everyone to hold a minute of silence for a dead raver, drawing thousands of people to a standstill, not an easy feat when most were soaring on Ecstasy and impatient to carry on with their night, but the DJ's voice was so solemn he managed to press the pause button for an entire minute, lording over everyone like an urban warlock, and then gradually, very gradually, after that long minute of silence was achieved, he introduced a mournful track with a foghorn in it, and the Belgian or wherever he was from said he would never forget that moment as the tune crept into the stilled space and life re-entered, reanimating everything. In fact he'd written a short story, 'A Minute of Silence for the Dead Raver', he'd never published anything in his life, he said, but two days after the party he sat down and wrote it, and ever since our conversation I'd wondered whether someday I would open a magazine and there it would be, and though the young man's face and voice and everything about him but his gloves had vanished from memory, the story of the dead raver survived.

As I continued my stroll the corridors began to feel less welcoming, the floor oddly aslant, the fluorescent lights bright enough to X-ray our interiors, the doors devoid of the earlier symmetry that helped fit them into doorways, now impossible to wedge shut. The result was so disorienting I nearly bumped into an elderly patient in her hospital gown being led by her maid in a pink-and-white uniform. Caked in make-up, the woman looked like an ageing actress who'd strayed from her dressing room, and she gripped her maid's arm as though this were the only person she trusted in the world, the person to whom, unbeknownst to her family, she would be leaving her fortune.

Moments after encountering this pair – the woman's eyes searched mine as we crossed paths and she smiled faintly – I came upon what I realised I'd been looking for, albeit at a distance: the figure in the wheelchair. A nurse stood by her side and, upon seeing me, waved me over. I glanced around to confirm I was the person she was addressing and walked towards them, there at the end of the corridor beside a potted palm tree and its serrated shadow, and once I was within hearing range the nurse asked whether I spoke any English, to which I replied yes, yes I did, while taking in the face that had come into focus: sharp eyes, stern mouth, heavy brow, shoulder-length hair in coppery red.

Thank heavens for that, said the patient in a German accent. Please tell the nurse I want to go outside for a cigarette, only one, I've been imprisoned here for days and I'm losing my mind, they must grant me five minutes of fresh air, five minutes with a cigarette, I don't even have to smoke the entire one, half will do.

Word for word, I translated.

But she's in here for pneumonia.

Yes, yes, the woman dismissed the nurse's words, I've had *pulmonía* many times, it's nothing to worry about.

She can't go out. She has to stay indoors. Hospital rules. And she definitely cannot smoke.

I translated back, aware of my own desire for one now.

The woman stomped her feet, large and slippered, on the metal ledge of the wheelchair and glowered up at us both as though we were equally to blame.

Voices. Hastening steps. A gurney hurtling down the corridor. Elsewhere in the wing, an emergency. Here there was no emergency, not even urgency, simply an urge that sought satisfaction.

The woman was now staring down at the floor. An impasse had been reached. She'd shut me out. I murmured goodnight in English and then Spanish. Only the nurse replied.

What was a German woman with pneumonia, or perhaps she was Swiss or Austrian, doing in a hospital in Mexico City all on her own, I wondered the following morning. Had she disembarked from a cruise ship or recently moved to Mexico or been abandoned while on holiday? That evening once the doctor on call had finished her rounds I set out on another stroll, this time heading straight for the corridor, my impatience reined in only by the drip. And very soon I glimpsed her, hunched in her wheelchair, a blanket over her shoulders. Tonight she was alone, there was no hovering nurse, though I sensed she was still under the command of a green uniform, unable to dispel its cloud of NO. As I approached I heard another mumbled request for a cigarette, and found myself asking whether she even had any with her at the hospital. Of course she did, she always travelled with a carton, she'd left it at the hotel but had a pack in the coat she'd been wearing when they'd brought her in, and by the way, her lungs were much stronger than yesterday, couldn't I hear, no more crinkling no more rattling, she could breathe in deeply and inhale more air, yes, the air travelled farther down than it had only twenty-four hours ago.

She fixed me with her gaze, its severity intensified by the dark eyes and prominent brow, and again I had to deny her what she most wanted and tell her I couldn't be of help, I too was a patient and had no influence, no authority, in fact the nurses hardly paid any attention to me.

From where I stood I had a good view of her hair, the silvery roots tapering into copper, and speculated as to when it had last been dyed.

I commented on her English, how exceptional it was (heavily accented but error-free), to which she replied with a note of exasperation that she'd been living in London for many years. I live in London too, I replied. She looked surprised, I thought, yet didn't comment on the fact. We then established that we both lived in the north-east of the city, in fact within walking distance of one another, less than four bus stops apart.

That's the thing, she said, you can live round the corner from someone for years and yet your paths never cross, unless thrown together by unusual circumstance.

Prompted by this coincidence, she told me her name: Wilhelmina.

And revealed she was staying on the floor above, reserved for heart and lung ailments. She preferred my floor, which focused on recovery, you felt its optimism as soon as you emerged from the lift, whereas her floor cultivated a near deathly silence. Glancing at my bandaged hand, she asked why I was there.

Two fractures, one in the thumb and one in a metacarpal, and lots of splintered bone. My parents' Alsatian had bitten me. And then, coming to his defence: Alsatians are fiercely intelligent and therefore grow skittish with age.

Enlightenment comes at a cost, she laughed, her laughter gruff and cavernous before mutating into a prolonged cough. Well, trips take unforeseen turns, she said once she'd stopped coughing, yours with your dog bite and mine with my lungs, although the pneumonia is less of a surprise.

She rarely travelled beyond Europe, she explained, hesitant to journey so far, but had always wanted to visit Mexico. An invitation to a convention was her chance. From the airplane the city looked monstrous, sprawling voraciously in every direction, nothing like the map of the Aztec capital of Tenochtitlán Dürer had admired in a woodcut in Vienna in 1524, declaring it afterwards the perfect metropolis (yet by the time he'd seen this woodcut, I could have told her, the city it depicted had been razed).

After giving her talk to a half-empty auditorium she had slipped away to the Museum of Anthropology, the place of her dreams. And it lived up to them. The museum was as violent and magisterial as she'd always imagined, bristling with skulls and snakes and jaguars. But the most extraordinary sculpture of all was a human heart carved from green stone, unlike the mineral grey of the others: it had a face, eyes, eyebrows and fangs, and emitted as much malice as the most sanguinary gods. Pulled into its orbit she stood pressed up to the glass and only after a few minutes managed to tear herself away. Next she went to stand in front of the Aztec stone calendar, where a group of young Italians took turns posing with a camera, and then on to

Coatlicue, she of the serpent skirt. It was there that the tightness in her chest began to set in, from one moment to the next it was as though an obsidian dagger had been plunged into her lungs and the stone calendar marked the last of her days, and with difficulty she dragged herself into the main courtyard, resting for several minutes on the edge of the pond by a giant conch shell she'd never have the strength to blow into, and finally towards the exit, the fine spray from the indoor waterfall reminding her she was still in the land of the living. A taxi brought her back to her hotel, where she arrived so shaky and feverish the people at reception immediately called an ambulance.

After this breathless monologue Wilhelmina paused for a moment and produced two bread rolls from under her robe, she'd asked for extras since the hospital portions were so small and how could they expect one to go for so many hours between meals, she said, before tearing off a chunk with her teeth. She was driven by an insatiable appetite, a nurse later told me, and would insist on two trays at mealtimes, a rare thing for pneumonia patients but not the German woman in room 423, who seemed to eat more than all the other patients combined. I watched her eat, her manners an unusual blend of savagery and etiquette. The first roll, then the second.

Once done, she resumed.

My son, on the other hand, he hardly eats a thing, he's a bit scatty and adrift, it's nothing to worry about, only the occasional gloomy spell that ails him, he hasn't found his path but I tell myself it's only a matter of time. He's now in his mid-thirties and still waiting for a bit of direction. He offered to fly out here but I told him absolutely not, he'd probably get lost on his way to the airport. Today the doctors mentioned some sort of surgical intervention but under no circumstances am I going to let anyone come near me, someone must convince them they are holding me here against my will, please tell them I need to return home, my son is alone in the house and that makes me nervous, I never know what he will get up to, and furthermore my feet will wither if I stay here much longer, they need movement, and my lungs will recover only once I leave this polluted city. Pneumonia's a frequent guest in my house and really nothing to be alarmed about, all I need is to be home again with someone who knows the ritual: flood my bedroom with eucalyptus oil, grant me fresh air and two cigs a day, and I'll mend in no time.

Her face changed scenery as she spoke, at moments dominated by a smile, then a frown, and then by something less distinct, and each time I started to formulate a portrait I was thrown off since the whole remained elusive, acquiring a particularly odd mien when she spoke about her recent visit to the Sonora Market, a place I'd been to only once myself. It was a locus of cruelty where every possible kind of animal was on offer, most creatures crammed into cages and destined for either food or Santería rituals, and after seeing a necklace of strung hummingbirds I knew I'd never return, wincing inwardly as Wilhelmina described her desire for a *pez diablo* skeleton, those suckermouth catfishes that when alive terrorise every other species in the lake and when dead transform into something demonic in their wizened incarnation.

She'd always wanted a *pez diablo*, she said, and once asked a friend to bring one back from Mexico – they were too fragile to post – but the friend refused to travel with something so evil in her suitcase, saying it would jinx the flight.

They may look like angry wretches that hate whatever's nourished by the sun but she found them endearing, especially their grimace and crested head and the way their spindly bones resembled ancient lace. At the Sonora Market it'd been easy to locate a stand that sold them, the woman had tried to convince her to buy three but she replied she only wanted one, and now this *pez diablo* was at the hotel. It occurred to her, as she spoke, that the chambermaid might mistake it for the skeleton of a fish she'd eaten and throw it out with the rubbish. If she could only recall the name of her hotel she would ask me to ring them and make sure her little beast was safe.

Her voice climbed an anxious note before dipping into another request for a cigarette. If you wheel me out now I'm sure no one will notice, not to the entrance but somewhere less visible, the back of the building, for instance, we should be fine if we go immediately, now is a good moment, let's go.

But I just stood there, what else was I to do, I wasn't defiant enough to risk the doctors' wrath or even that of the nurses, or perhaps it had more to do with my own twilight state, medication shaved the edge off of things and without an edge how were decisions to be made, in addition to which, I hadn't had any caffeine since the morning of the dog bite and with my senses dulled, most clarity and courage were gone.

It occurred to me to explain it would be impossible to manoeuvre the wheelchair with my bandaged hand, there'd be no way of pushing or angling it and my right hand simply wasn't strong enough to take full command. And once I told her that, holding up each hand to illustrate my point, she stopped treating me as a potential accomplice.

Once I was demoted to fellow invalid, only then, our conversation ventured into new territory, Wilhelmina pausing every so often to draw breath before rushing onwards.

She began by telling me about the last time she'd been hospitalised for pneumonia. Three years ago, in west London. The only distraction from the piercing chest pain was an extraordinary birdsong she heard once or twice a day, perhaps a blackbird or a robin. Its source was a mystery. Did the song enter through the wall or from outside or was there a poor bird trapped under her bed or in the wardrobe? There it was again. She finally asked a nurse, who explained that in the room next door lay a ninety-year-old man in a coma. This man had once been a famous birdsong impersonator in Ireland, in fact Ireland's most famous, he could imitate the call of any bird, and each day his family would play him his old recordings to see whether he might respond.

Here the walls are so thick, she said, gesturing vaguely, it would be impossible to hear sounds from a neighbouring room. We should be thankful for that. And as for these long empty corridors – ahead of us lay the dim stretch where a light continued to flicker and hiss – just think of what could be brought to life if only we had the right instruments, how we would benefit from this tension of space.

It was then that she told me about her collection. One of the greatest collections in the world, she said, of pre-cinema toys and instruments. You know, optical illusions and things like that. Someone once said that the German psyche has a tendency to endow the inanimate with a soul, and in my home that thought was illustrated one hundred times over. Just imagine: shelves and shelves of magic lanterns and peep boxes, long mirrors that returned sideshow reflections, zoetropes and phenakistoscopes, shadow puppets in every corner.

I tried, unsuccessfully, to imagine, my mind still on the comatose birdsong impersonator.

Do you even know what a magic lantern is?

I sensed she'd asked this question many times before. An old-fashioned device came to mind, figures that spun when the thing was given a whirl.

Does it spin?

No, that's a zoetrope, where you peer through the slits of a spinning cylinder and see images come alive. Or perhaps you're thinking of a phenakistoscope – discs that when spun also merge a sequence of images to create a sense of motion. Both beautiful forms of early animation. As for the magic lantern, my favourite of all, it casts images onto a wall or screen. If you've ever walked down Bloomsbury Way, which I imagine you have, you may have spotted one in the window of the Swedenborg bookshop . . . Once you've seen one you won't forget. I owned dozens of them: tin, wood, porcelain. Half were male in aura, squatting with their long lenses and beckoning confidence, always ready to pontificate, and the other half were female, a demure box into which a slide could be slipped, bringing the room to life. Of all the conjurors of reverie the magic lantern is perhaps the most basic, almost rudimentary. Its optics are no mystery. A box with a set of lenses and a light source. Sometimes the lantern anchors the magic, other times the magic grants the lantern flight, sometimes it is neither magic nor lantern, simply a dormant eye. When we're both back in London I can tell you more.

The prospect of meeting her again in an entirely different context, in another city, was more than a little thrilling, and I sensed in her too a quiet refusal of the lethargy that tried to impose itself there at the hospital.

I'd like that, I said.

I wish I could show you more than a lantern but there's little left of my collection. I once had a kingdom. For decades I scoured the flea markets, went to the fairs, engaged in long correspondences with other collectors, even people I didn't care for, and over the years I found things no one else had even dreamt existed. And I shared it all with my husband Jan, the gentle Dutchman they called him, who sailed rather briskly through my life. You'll see when you're older that currents quicken when you're happy . . . But I'm going on, as usual. Tell me about yourself. Begin with your name.

Flora, I replied, but at that very moment the nurse came to wheel her away, leaving my two syllables suspended in the air.

Who was I? Self-portraits must often be drawn in hospital beds, perhaps more accurately than in the outside world. Mine was hardly noteworthy. Early forties. Phlegmatic, melancholic, yet prone to occasional acts of daring, a flat line interrupted by the sudden jump. If pressed, probably more centripetal than centrifugal in nature. The hermit in me liked to stay home, the little vampire loved to step out. Sometimes they remained locked in battle for hours. Romances: plentiful in number, short in duration. I was drawn to the chilliness of some people and to the warmth of others. *People are not composed of your thoughts,* a counsellor once said to me. Yes they are, I'd insisted, and had never been able to stop constructing stories in my head, especially at times when reality fell short of expectations. Friends came and went. I preferred animals to most fellow beings and often wished I'd been born another species. The main constant seemed to be my home, three gusty rooms on the top floor of a house belonging to a retired couple and their cats. After a degree in history I'd yearned to do something contemporary and creative – painter, writer, photographer, dancer – and sought part-time jobs while attempting to develop my skills. But nothing came naturally (you have to believe in yourself at least a little, I realised, in order to create), and I was endlessly haunted by a Manuel Manilla engraving of a skeleton seated at a table with all sorts of tools of trade laid out before it: scissors, saw, hammer, trowel, comb, knife, revolver, books, wooden foot, and, teetering over its shoulder as a warning to that boundless community of the adrift, a miniature sarcophagus. Someone had later added the caption: *Jack of all trades, master of none.*

Just as I was on the verge of handing myself over to full-time poverty and despair I took a metals course at an arts centre and discovered I was very good at something: polishing. Ever since I was a girl I've been drawn to shiny things, *little magpie* my mother would call me, not because I ever nicked other children's toys but because my eye and hands would gravitate towards whatever sparkled, a sequin scarf or a glittery hair clip, and I always held to the idea that most things had the potential of being enhanced, of being given a small lift out of their matte existence. After hours and hours of practice – friends would lend me their silver and I'd return it, transformed – I became a polisher at a jewellery shop in Soho. Our little shop was the perfect sanctuary after years of disappointment. And not only was I a polisher, but a master polisher, and to be master of anything is something to be proud of.

Furthermore, polishing is not an art to be taken lightly. We add shadow or lustre to an object, remove some of its history or stealthily add a make-believe one, and if Wilhelmina were to ask again who I was I would omit the dead ends and mention only the silver.

Aren't you dying to come home, my mother said when the doctors announced I'd have to stay a few extra days for a final intervention, your room has been waiting and Diogenes is calm, but I told her I felt content where I was and not yet ready to move. In fact, I had settled in even more; someone had taken note of our nightly conversations and left out a stool. Wilhelmina and I were now at the same height.

When I arrived that evening her wheelchair was facing the stool and for the first time we were able to look directly into each other's eyes, moving between seriousness and sympathy before one of us, Wilhelmina, naturally, began the conversation. The stool on which I was sitting, she said, reminded her of stools at the preventorium where she'd spent a summer as a girl, a place in the French mountains where children who had yet to show symptoms were sent after testing positive for tuberculosis, a kind of antechamber of disease. Those stools were wooden, more old-fashioned than this one, but seeing any stool sent her back to that strange summer. The preventorium building – stone walls and pillars, high windows and rational arches – had previously been a Cistercian abbey. And, in keeping, the place harboured a past reverence for silence, the infirm children forbidden to speak at certain hours of the day, as well as for agricultural labour, and the more robust individuals were asked to till the land with little shovels, a symbolic gesture more than anything since the holes they dug were too shallow and irregular for proper cultivation. She remembered the refectory for its chequered floors and chilly restraint, and the nuns who presided over meals from the head of every long table, their faces cut from the same stone as that of the abbey. The older nuns would communicate with one another via a monastic sign language that only deepened the atmosphere of austerity, and the sense that other-worldly secrets were being traded and withheld.

The children slept on hard beds with iron railings and starchy sheets, shabby stuffed animals on rotation; you never knew which evening you would find one sitting on your pillow when you returned from supper. Wilhelmina's best friend had been a girl named Heidi with whom she'd play hopscotch in the courtyard and search for lame black beetles on the dusty paths. They had the same pageboy haircut, the same yen for adventure. One night they snuck into the immense kitchen and watched a sickly mouse leaping out of a vat of soup, its fur and whiskers coated in a milky substance. Everything was elegant, bucolic, and quietly languishing under the spectre of death.

After that summer Wilhelmina's family moved to a little Bavarian town surrounded by the peaks of the Vorarlberg. Still at an age when correspondence seemed like a grown-up endeavour, she and Heidi lost touch. Over the years she'd sometimes wondered what had become of her friend, whether she had survived. Some children became preventorium regulars or progressed to the sanatorium; those whose lungs strengthened over time would look back on their visits as a misty episode unaligned with the rest of life. Decades passed. And then eight years ago, Wilhelmina had been hospitalised for acute pneumonia. She was at a fair in Lyon and rushed to the nearest hospital, where she was put in a room with a woman suffering from advanced dementia. The woman's gown kept unravelling and she no longer seemed to recognise her husband or children, straying from her bed to be gently led back by a nurse. Despite the vacancy in her eyes Wilhelmina identified her instantly, her hunches confirmed when the husband addressed her by name. It was Heidi of the dust-path beetles and the vat-vaulting mouse. Here she was, before her. Two childhood friends, sharing the same hospital room, what were the chances of that, their beds two metres apart, separated by a dark blue curtain and decades of experiences. Every now and then, lungs permitting, Wilhelmina tried to speak to her, but the woman met her words with bewilderment. It was a conversation between a fever and an absence, and in her fevered state Wilhelmina relived moments from their past and for an instant they were again children, she with compromised yet functioning lungs and Heidi with a functioning mind. She tried to explain who she was to the family but they didn't appear to understand what she was saying. When she awoke from her fever, the bed beside hers lay empty.

I hadn't realised hospital visits could be so eventful, I said, first a birdsong impersonator and then a childhood friend. They didn't seem eventful at the time, Wilhelmina replied, only now that I tell you about them, two interesting neighbours in a succession of bland ones. And I can't say every stay leads to transformation, in fact none of them have, but they do give you time to think about your life as you orbit it from outside.

The next day while the nurse measured my vital signs and the doctor and *infectólogo* inspected my hand, exchanging a few cryptic words as they turned it over, I tried blocking out the discomfort by thinking about Wilhelmina's various memories, all somewhat outlandish, and wondered whether a few were concocted, anything was possible, and in order to test how easy it was I attempted my own imaginative leaps, transporting myself to that mountain sanatorium somewhere in Europe, its outer strata lined with deckchairs and its inner strata with philosophical conversations, not to mention the handsome gaunt characters pacing the corridors and the friendships forged over X-rays. Yet they all suffered from similar ailments, whereas here we each had our own symptoms, treatment and trajectory, and my every flight of fancy was promptly grounded with the arrival of the lunch or dinner tray.

The storm that afternoon was unusual for Mexico's rainy season, materialising within minutes rather than mounting in pressure. I'd watched its sudden appearance from the hospital window, then listened to the percussion of hail on the sill. Wilhelmina had observed it too, its movements and its appetite. How many storms had been painted from memory, the confluence of many storms, storms that'd been brewing for years, each element sourced from a different drama, expanding until they finally joined? Earlier in life she had been able to witness the force of nature from up close. Her house in Germany was situated on the river and she'd spend much of the day on the adjoining terrace observing the current. She and Jan would sit there for hours, each in their favourite chair, armed with coffee and cigarettes, and revel in the tension of the river, particularly at night, thick and dark as it coursed past. *The tension of the river.* All around them lay a countryside that was growing more and more industrialised, advancing implacably as steel mills pushed out the native birds and bats, yet their place in it seemed fixed, and they enjoyed this sense of fixity, however illusory, as the water flowed by.

Most people only acknowledge the presence of nature when it threatens their lives or livelihoods, she said, when it swells in significance and spills out of the parameters we've assigned it. Only when it agitates our minds and redraws the boundaries. Then we take notice. Well, I was never one of those people. From the moment I moved into our home, I watched the river, kept an eye on it. In all its forms, all its moods, all its shades, it existed. But then Jan drowned – fell or jumped, we'll never know – and it became a living tomb. After that day I would sometimes glimpse thick curls in the churning water.

Once more she gesticulated as she spoke, her blanket slipping off her shoulders, and commanded the space so fully and confidently I forgot she was in a wheelchair. A nurse appeared, readjusted the blanket, left.

She'd met Jan at a scientific instrument fair in Antwerp. He had a tiny stall, easily overlooked, a one-man enterprise. As she stood contemplating the jumble of magnifying glasses, eyeglasses, vintage thermometers and barometers, none accompanied by a price tag, none displayed at their best angle, she suspected he was too attached to his wares to ever part with anything. This was confirmed when he gave a brief demonstration of an eighteenth-century microscope to two men before hastily returning it to its box and ignoring them when they enquired into the price. She listened as he then mumbled the origins of a tinted daguerreotype, made in Java in the early 1840s. He had sad eyes behind round glasses and wavy straw-coloured hair, and reminded her of the Dutch lens- and clock-makers of the seventeenth century. As she leaned in to catch every word, she realised this was a person with whom she could share her collection. Eight months later, they married.

Their combined collection included illusions created by movement, illusions created by a shift in illumination, and illusions created in some other way. He was more interested in the science, she in the illusion itself. Together they had nearly 40,000 objects. Two-thirds of the collection lived in a warehouse but the other third occupied every surface, cupboard, corner of their home. Jan often dreamt of being free of everything. *We will never be free*, he would say, or *I will never be a free man*, but she dismissed it as melodrama. Yet sometimes even she would see every instrument as a cage with an illusion trapped inside. Sometimes even she felt like going around the room feeding them oil and electricity. And she couldn't help feeling that every single thing harboured the same indistinct fear, engraved in its very parts, of modern technology. Her wish was to protect them all.

Unplanned, they had a son.

Nachtfalter. Folder of night. Is what she called him. Jan, not the son. Night butterfly, wild moth. There was something carved about his face, and he would occupy spaces by flattening against a wall or sitting immobile in a chair, arms folded, barely there. So tranquil, so removed, you hardly noticed him in a room. She imagined him decades later: now an old faun, fading into the domestic vegetation.

She paused, as if thinking back on the image.

Hunched in her wheelchair, shoulders stooped over the past.

I told her about the giant black moths I would see papered to the walls and ceilings of my childhood. Completely flat like paper cut-outs or silhouettes, a kind of Gothic origami or an anti-Matisse. Their true colour was only revealed by a camera's flash: dark brown. Unlike other moths these didn't draw in their capes when in repose but remained with outspread wings, motionless, for days. One never saw them any more.

She stared at my mouth while I spoke as though willing it to shut. Annoyed, perhaps, that I'd interrupted. Yet I sensed this was the scrutiny she gave everything, her gaze travelling from my lips to my forehead, and once I'd stopped speaking, her eyes coming to rest on mine, she returned to her memories. Her first ever collection was of live beetles, followed by an obsession with minerals after a visit to a steel mill with her grandfather when she was eight. Next came fossils, gathered from a local quarry. Over time the beetles multiplied into a city of industrious scarabs whose plans and activities outgrew their terrarium, and one evening at dusk she lifted the lid and watched their blue-black armoured bodies fill the sky.

Seeing another tenuous moment for connection, I mentioned I worked in a jewellery shop. We dealt mainly in silver, I said, but a few of our rings had stones. The silver cat ring could be fitted with diamond or emerald eyes, for example, and one of the skulls had opals. Our eye rings were prosthetic, the veins painted in afterwards, and we even had a ring with an eye infection. The shop lay directly above our workshop. She should come by, she would like the place, especially since we had many skulls, though tamer than the ones at the Museum of Anthropology. I offered to polish any jewellery of hers at no cost.

That's kind of you, Flora (a jolt – she'd remembered my name), but I don't need anything polished, in fact I like a bit of chiaroscuro and verdigris. But I might just buy something, she said before again returning to her memories, committed to the path she'd started out on. These early collections were rehearsals for the main collection of my life, she went on, which was launched the day I walked into a magic shop in Barcelona, set up long ago by the legendary

Catalan magician Partagás, and was shown a pack of thaumatropes. That's where it all began, with paper discs that when spun merge the images on either side: a parrot + an empty cage = a caged bird; a woman in bed + a perching imp = incubus; a prancing horse + a fluted pole = a carousel animal.

Have you ever seen *those* before? she asked, unrelenting.

I shook my head, trying to imagine what woman + wheelchair would equal.

You should have visited me when I still had my collection, she said, as though this had been an option, there would've been a great deal to show you. My home may have seemed like a sea of jumbled objects, but I knew where everything was and could locate any item within minutes. At night I'd mentally wander the rooms, that's how I sent myself to sleep, though sometimes it got me too stirred up and I'd have to reroute my thoughts towards something more humdrum, like who would be taking a parcel to the post office or replacing the bulb on the terrace. But my thoughts would always return to my objects, after all, even in the dark they somehow continued to illustrate, for me, the persistence of vision – a contested concept, I know – and within it, anyway, lay something deeper, which is what I learned over time: that human emotions are repeated, we have but a finite number, and watching my instruments in motion and the gestures they captured I saw how the same gestures are repeated over the centuries in one vast theatre of the soul.

As she spoke, woman and wheelchair merged into a hybrid in front of me, and I struggled to banish the thaumatrope image from my mind in order to focus on what she was saying, especially since in the last few moments her expression had clouded over.

She would never forget the morning she woke up and, as though to punish herself for events beyond her control, decided to get rid of everything. Jan had drowned six months before. She was still struggling through the days, impossible to focus on anything. There were occasions when there was hardly any food in the house and her son ate crisps and olives for breakfast. It was time to start a new life, unburdened, in England, a country she had always loved. Jan wouldn't have cared, in fact he would have supported her – he'd found the shadow puppets too slight, the peep boxes too cunning, the zoetropes vertiginous. There were two choices: she could hand everything over to a museum and keep the collection intact, the dream, of course, of every collector, or sell it off, casting it into that immense diaspora of optical illusion.

Another pause.
Am I boring you?
Not at all.
In the end no museum wanted to pay me, they wanted everything for free, so I chose to sell it off, yes, I sold off nearly everything, except my favourite lantern, a simple lantern, probably the least sophisticated of them all, yet from the moment I encountered it I felt it had to be mine, and have kept it close ever since. But even my favourite lantern couldn't console me when I watched the collection go.

I don't think I'll ever be faced with something like that. I own very few things and am hardly attached to anything.
Not even people?
I try not to get attached to them either, I said.

She was now looking into my face so intently I had the impulse, that instant, to spill out my life to her, or at least try to convey some of its tangled landscape, and would have probably done so if the nurse who'd readjusted her blanket weren't now walking towards us, the arrival of a green uniform announcing the end of the evening's conversation. The woman unlocked the two brakes on the wheelchair's hind wheels, one stuck and needed to be given a kick, and Wilhelmina half smiled a farewell before being steered away. Back in my room it was impossible not to look upon the objects around me in a changed light: the looming television, the telephone, the miniature cactus on the night table, the drip bent over my bed like an arthritic nurse, the pump of gel at the entrance marking the boundary between sickness and health, health and contagion, contagion and imaginary malady. Patients came and went yet all these objects remained, as indifferent to the cleaner who daily mopped the immaculate floor as to any human misery unfolding within those walls. Here in the hospital each one of us was torn from the material things that defined us in life. Our props scarcely varied from room to room. All the ornaments that had ever passed through my hands or Wilhelmina's ceased to matter; without design, we had all become a bit more holy through this imposed renunciation of riches.

Along with cartons of thick nectary juice there was the ubiquitous bread roll, white and insipid with an indentation down the middle. Soft and malleable to begin with, it would quickly harden if neglected for too long. I rarely ate mine and began saving them for Wilhelmina, bringing her one each evening. Handing her the rolls also allayed something further, like I was handing over the day's frustration, compressed into a tiny white oval. Sometimes she would take a few bites, chewing pensively before she began to speak, or else she'd hold it intact for the duration of our meeting. *A nutritional pyramid* was how one doctor described the meal tray, yet I couldn't see any geometrical shape, only deconstructed ones, and it seemed as though the eggs and vegetables had checked in with severe anaemia.

    I'd just wrapped my morning roll in a napkin and laid it on the bedside table when a headache began to set in. It must have been the potent intravenous antibiotic or so many hours recumbent or the strain of listening to someone so closely that the muscles in my neck and shoulders had gone stiff. Whatever the cause, the pain was excruciating. Until then I'd worried it was Wilhelmina who was straining herself, rarely pausing, breathless as she rushed along, and I hadn't paid much attention to my own body apart from the vague area of my hand. She had spoken about a certain tension of space. And the tension of the river. If I were to speak about any sort of tension it would undoubtedly be a tension of the head. Headaches had featured in my life since childhood, setting in towards the end of the school hours and taking full possession on the bus home so that by the time I returned I often had to skip lunch and go lie down in my room. They would appear in London too but I now had strong medication to thwart their progress. Unlike the shattering headache Zeus once experienced, a howl so loud it echoed across the earth and was only alleviated when Hephaestus split his head open and a fully-formed Athena leapt out, nothing unusual, nothing bold or magnificent, ever emerged from my pain.

    I asked the nurse for a sumatriptan but she gave me liquid analgesic instead, a chilly current introduced through the drip. Half an hour later, the pain hadn't diminished. And the more I willed it away, the worse it became. In my room someone had drawn the curtains yet the Mexican sun fought its way in, organised into a white frame around the window: nightfall was still a few hours away. How would Wilhelmina react if I didn't show up, I wondered, would she be puzzled or annoyed or indifferent, would she wait for a while or ask someone to wheel her back to her floor? I gripped the bed control and tried out different angles, forty-five degrees and ninety and other measures in between. The ideal position was elusive or non-existent. Fully horizontal I felt my head would explode but too vertical brought its own measure of discomfort. Eventually a young nurse, someone I hadn't seen before, returned my bed to the slight tilt with which it'd started out.

    By 8:30 the worst of my headache had lifted, replaced by a lingering thrum. When I told Wilhelmina how I'd spent the day she said that a splitting headache meant you felt torn or split between two things. Would you say that's the way you're feeling now? she asked. I don't know, I replied, aware it was the sort of question I would have an answer for only afterwards.

My son gets headaches too, she said, before lapsing into a torrent of coughing.

Once she'd finished coughing, I handed her my roll.

My poor son . . . whom you must meet, by the way, when we return to London . . .

Ever more intrigued, I decided it was a good moment to ask a question that could cover a lot of ground, potentially: and how did this son of hers spend his days?

Oh, Max is between jobs, she said, folding her kerchief, and spends a lot of time at home . . . He used to work at an NHS surgery, but was asked to leave since he often showed up late. He loves putting things off till the last minute, always one more cup of tea when he should be walking out the door. Even with German and Dutch parents he's always been a disaster when it comes to punctuality . . . It has nothing to do with a disregard for clocks or time, simply a desire to tempt fate and see how far he can take things. He has very nice eyes and hair, my son, she added as if deciding to paint a more alluring portrait, and despite being a bit shy he had a band when he was younger, with his best friend Leon. It was actually quite good. They played at school fairs and even a few venues until Leon went north to study medicine. Sometimes I think he should pursue a career in music, if it's not too late . . . Well, he's still waiting for his swerve. We should each have our own swerve in life, that moment when we defy our nature and deviate from the path we find ourselves on, a cleavage between before and after. *Everything comes into being as a result of the swerve. Nothing new emerges from keeping to a straight line . . .* My son is still waiting for his swerve.

It was then that I told her about my father. Over the last few days I'd had a growing urge to share something of my own, and now that she mentioned this thing called a swerve, it seemed like a fitting word to describe what he'd done. I intended to mention him briefly, there was no need to elaborate, but something came over me and I found myself sharing more. I spoke at length and in a hurry, as if under pressure to reassemble him before the evening was over, cobbling together a man made of spare parts as I told her how he'd worked in the tall tower of an electricity company called Luz y Fuerza and how he'd been missing a molar and would complain at night that his mouth felt draughty and how he'd never learned to drive but loved reading maps. His favourite writer was a Russian revolutionary named Victor Serge and he had all of his books on a shelf but never let anyone go near them. My mother used to say he was a lamb in temperament but his stomach growled constantly, you could hear it whenever the room was silent, always growling, and I often imagined a large animal inside that longed to roam but was rarely given the chance. He was from the north of England, my father, and had come to Mexico in his mid-twenties to work, met my mother at a cafe and stayed on, and despite no longer being in my life it was thanks to him I could live in London.

And finally, I told her about the Sunday afternoon he disappeared. And the countless times I'd tried to conjure him afterwards, desperate to bring him back even if the sight would have sent my mother into heart failure. She emptied his wardrobe and donated all of his possessions to a stray dog charity, yet I managed to salvage his sweaters and wore them often and with mixed feelings, the wool so impregnated with naphthalene that years later it still managed to scare away even the English moths and the only holes were historical, courtesy of Mexican moths from the eighties. How many incantations did I perform in their bedroom when no one else was home, in the very room where years later the dog would bite me, addressing photographs that continued to languish in family albums, this man whose image reigned over everything in silent, fragile ambivalence, at least during the period between his disappearance and the arrival of my stepfather, whose presence put an end to any possibility of a prodigal return.

Upon reaching the end of my story I turned to look at Wilhelmina. Her eyes were closed, her head dropped onto a shoulder, the blanket slipping from her chest, which rose and fell almost imperceptibly. I did not know at what point she had drifted off. Perhaps I'd gone on for too long, added too much detail. Wilhelmina? I said softly. No response. I thought of saying her name more loudly but the sight was so moving, all that pluckiness brought to a lull, I decided not to disturb. Yet I couldn't help feeling a twinge of vexation given the nature of what I'd just shared, and how attentively I had been listening to her.

The nurses say you have made a friend here.

My mother removed her scarf as she settled into her spot on the sofa.

An older German woman, she added with a note of suspicion.

Yes, I have made a new friend.

And who is this person?

She used to be a collector.

Of what?

Old toys.

And where does she live?

In London. Actually, not far from me.

So she's a tourist?

She came for a conference.

What sort of conference?

A conference on old toys, I think.

A conference on old toys? But who is she, Flora?

Her name is Wilhelmina, I replied, as though the name were to explain everything.

And what sort of name is that?

The other patients I'd glimpsed early on seemed to have vanished from their thresholds but from time to time a face would emerge from behind a door or a new arrival could be seen making exploratory rounds with nurse and drip, and one night the elderly woman with heavy make-up reappeared and walked past us in loops, somehow enacting the repetition of our days. After the nurse had wheeled Wilhelmina to her spot and walked off, handing over her share of responsibility, my friend turned to me and said, as though finishing a thought, but sometimes life still throws up its gems and takes you by surprise. That's what makes it worth living. Like this visit to Mexico.

After the Sonora Market she had gone to the Lagunilla, which like any flea market in a foreign country shows you a more hidden side. Next to a display of second-hand mirrors, trumpets and guitars, some quite beautiful, she'd come upon a more familiar setting: an antiquarian selling items he'd acquired decades ago in Utrecht, Antwerp and Berlin. His wife was now very ill, he said, and he wanted to sell everything. Among the objects laid out on the table were a zoetrope and several boxes of magic lantern slides. The zoetrope wasn't in terribly good condition, it tilted shakily and several of the paper strips had torn, so she focused her attention on the glass slides. One by one she opened the cardboard boxes and sifted through them. Jet-lagged and confused, she set thirty aside, then put a few back, then a few more, and, deciding that she really didn't need more slides, she still had a number at home and, for that matter, only one lantern with which to project them, she returned the rest to their boxes, except for one: a hand-coloured photographic slide of Empress Carlota, standing in the gardens of Castle Bouchout. Beyond Mexico and Maximilian her life had continued for several lonely decades. The slide wasn't in perfect condition, some of the paint had flaked and there was a crack in the upper right-hand corner, but she could see it was unusual. And it filled her with existential horror.

My thoughts began to drift – to history class, to family walks in Chapultepec Park, to my father's interest in the doomed emperor rather than his wife – as Wilhelmina carried on. She was now telling me about how Carlota's nerves were already frayed upon arriving in Mexico, her ears tortured by the screeching of the carriage wheels, and each time Maximilian descended from the royal carriage to inspect some botanical specimen he'd glimpsed from the window she would anxiously call him back. And then she told me how decades later, in the family castle in Belgium, in the twilight of her years and in the depths of her madness, Carlota was said to lay out her favourite dresses on chairs and speak to each one in a separate language, as though they were ladies-in-waiting from different chapters of her life.

Wilhelmina seemed to know unusual details about these figures who'd formed a significant albeit dramatically abbreviated part of our history – the extravagant mission to establish an Austrian-style empire in Mexico had failed, and Maximilian was led to the firing squad – and I let her speak without interruption, trying to understand her fascination with the troubled empress. A nurse was coming towards us. Time to say goodnight. Only then did I remember the bread roll I'd been holding the entire length of our conversation. It had grown soft again in my hands. I held it out, uncertain Wilhelmina would still find it appealing, and watched her devour it as she was wheeled away.

Dawn was at the window when they came for me, my hand wasn't healing as well as they'd hoped and the doctors had decided on a final intervention, and in the operating theatre I listened once more to the anaesthetist enquiring whether I wanted rum, vodka or tequila, this time I'd prepared a reply but he knocked me out before I could utter it, and when I awoke I was back in my room, my hand swaddled in a thick, tight bandage. A nurse was bending over me, her face drifting in and out of focus. She asked whether I was hungry, I said no but she brought the lunch tray and set it on a table in case I changed my mind.

Minutes later she returned to the room, this time to announce, breathlessly, that there was a surprise on its way. Before I could ask what kind of surprise since I generally didn't like them, two painted faces with red plastic noses and carnival mouths appeared at the door. Uncertain how to react I smiled in their direction, invitation enough for them to come bounding into my room and make their jaunty way over to my bed.

The hospital clowns had finished early in the children's ward and decided to do a quick tour of the other floors. Surely everyone needed cheering up, not only children. The male clown looked around fifty, the woman in her mid-thirties. She had oversized shoes with yellow flower buckles, his were black and flapping like old boats, and they both wore polka-dot suits with shiny buttons. I watched as they flailed their arms about, writing nonsense words in the air, distant cousins of the Chapulín Colorado. The man pretended to trip over something on the floor and nearly fell into my food tray. He then picked up the phone and prattled into the receiver, opened the wardrobe door and greeted someone inside. He glanced behind the curtains and under the bed, greeting people in those places too. For a few minutes, the room was filled with imaginary beings.

In all their bagginess, in all their boisterousness, the clowns tried to summon a reaction. I thought of smiling again yet feared what a second smile would encourage. For the first time in hospital, I felt captive. Captive to the mobile, the vigorous, the robust, and with my tightly bandaged aching hand I began to feel I was witnessing all the structure and order that held the place together come undone, corridors unzipped, walls torn apart at the seams. The clowns made everything elastic, so elastic, the architecture expanding and contracting on the spot. I felt grateful for this moment of liberation. And then a little annoyed.

The female clown had stopped by the foot of my bed to readjust her nose. She removed it, tightened the elastic, and quickly slipped it back over her head, and in that brief act I glimpsed something like desolation, the sorrow in the building transferred rather than dispelled, and the more I studied her while her colleague danced around uncontainedly, the more I watched her clown essence dissolve. Nose back in place, and without glancing again in my direction, she whispered something to her colleague and they both left the room in steps less jaunty and exaggerated than those with which they'd entered.

To anaesthetise the moment. That was the clowns' mission, *to anaesthetise the moment*, the nurse who brought me dinner said without further explanation, though I struggled to see what she meant since their visit had not anaesthetised a thing. The clowns had only made me more aware of my confinement. Make me another date with the real anaesthetist, knock me out to the hilt. I was impatient to hear whether Wilhelmina had received a visit from the red noses too and what her response would have been but when I arrived at our usual place that evening I was startled to find only one figure at the end of the corridor, standing beside the space where the wheelchair would park. Your friend asks that you come to her room tonight, said her nurse as soon as I was within hearing range, reading the alarm on my face.

Wilhelmina had not been wrong: her floor cultivated a deathly atmosphere. The air reeked of cotton and alcohol. It rang with electronic beeps and suspense. These sounds and smells of critical care were punctuated only by the occasional tortuous cough. Outside most of the rooms sat oxygen tanks and mysterious machines, and apart from two doctors who walked past muttering in anxious tones I didn't see anyone as I followed the nurse down a corridor. She led me into a room, dark but for the light of a table lamp. I took tiny steps, careful not to catch my drip on a corner of furniture, and was directed towards an empty chair.

They've sent over my things from the hotel and say I can fly home soon, a voice said, so I thought I'd put on a show for you.

The wheelchair was stationed in front of a table, the table that held the lamp, and beside this lamp was a tin instrument, somewhere in size between a coffee grinder and a sewing machine, with a long lens and chimney. It was the first time I'd seen a magic lantern. But I scarcely had time to inspect it before it came alive, a glowing eye in the dark face of the room. Saturated colours poured out of its lens, colours molten and luminous like those of a stained-glass window, injecting the empty wall with life.

 A nun clutching a scarlet-tipped dagger, her wailing mouth a gash of red.

 A skeleton in a plumed hat. His eyes move to the left, to the right.

 A hare in Prussian blue, with jutting ribs and diaphanous ears.

 A head of Medusa, chartreuse green, with serpents coiling out.

 A lunar eclipse framed by indigo clouds. Otherworldly faces emerge in their midst.

 A procession of hooved creatures with lute, cymbal and guitar. They raise and lower their instruments, the music marking their step.

 A Venetian funeral: three gondolas cloaked in black, three black lines disturbing the turquoise water.

The interior of a grotto: eerie blue lake, stalactites. On the surface of the water floats a small boat, unoccupied.

Glowing, acrobatic angels above a shepherd's hut.

Even more deeply saturated colours poured out of the lantern as a medieval mood descended over the room.

Four oak trees, representing a wood. In this wood stands the figure of an archer. Grey tunic, rounded helmet, a pouch of arrows slung across his chest.

The same figure leaning over a turret. The arrow in his bow is drawn.

A close-up of his handsome face, his features look engraved.

The archer sits on a large rock, bow and arrows resting at his side. He is pensive, bathed in a blue-and-green marbled light.

Each image lingered on the wall for a number of seconds, accompanied by a clacking sound as Wilhelmina pulled out one slide and slid in the next, and the air grew thick with beings, ugly, beautiful and beguiling, beings that absorbed the heaviness and transformed it into coloured particles, and I too longed to shed the prosaic world of the ward and everything beyond it, to lose substance and dissolve in a beam of light. This dream of weightlessness was interrupted by soft laughter behind me. Several faces were peering in at the door, nurses who with childlike fascination had also been watching the new guests in the room.

The head of the Great Sphinx, the sun setting behind her haunches.

A soldier dreaming by the side of the road. A thought bubble over his head shows a scene of his wife and children back home.

A robed magician in his den. He waves his wand up and down. A procession of rats and toads and unidentifiable creatures flow out of his cauldron.

The figure of Robinson Crusoe gripping a rock as he watches his ship go down.

Wilhelmina then rose from the wheelchair and tilted the lantern up towards the ceiling to cast a painted typhoon rising from a misty sea. As though to clear the air, the way incense does in churches, of darker visions. A loud breathing filled the room, the breathing of overexertion, and I couldn't help thinking she was now exhaling the images, that they emerged from her lungs rather than from the lantern, every out breath producing more ectoplasmic ghouls.

And then one final image: a woman in a garden. Pale, caped and febrile. An unembellished projection in the dark. There in the garden alone with her thoughts. It didn't seem she – Carlota? – was aware of being photographed.

Wilhelmina collapsed into the wheelchair. Lantern off. Overhead light on.

No longer emitting reverie, the instrument retreated into its taciturn shell. And the nurses to standby, ahead in their thoughts and behind in their work. The hospital re-entered the room, the heaviness flooded back.

Cheeks flushed, eyes ablaze, Wilhelmina remained very still. Thank you so much, that was beautiful, really beautiful, I said, but she didn't seem to hear me.

It must have been shortly afterwards that the fever swept over me. The nurse who read out 39C seemed perplexed, after each of my surgeries the mercury hadn't risen, while the doctor on duty wondered out loud whether this was a new infection, the *infectólogo* reappearing like a soothsayer to herald the complication, or was it the strange play of light that'd started up in my room, a weird shadow play conducted by the trees outside, punctuated by flashbacks of a figure leaping towards me, a figure with gleaming eyes, 39 degrees, 39 micro gestures, human and animal, endlessly repeated.

Here she was, consulting an old volume or sitting solemnly in a chair, shoulders hunched as she puffed on a cigarette, and then she was gone, there she was, shivering on a street corner in Antwerp at dawn waiting for the old toy market to open, and then she was gone, there she was, studying constellations in the night sky, and then she was gone, here she was, prowling hospital corridors in a stately fog, a giant zoetrope spun round and round, revealing a scene, slicing it, another scene, another cut, all part of a great vanishing act, a great feat, possibly, of misdirection.

When I emerged from the fever I immediately sensed a change. Even before taking note of the nurse's stricken face and the way she paused with the breakfast tray, postponing the moment of its delivery. Had there been another earthquake? No, she said, and she made me wait till after she'd deposited the tray on a foldout table and peeled away the aluminium foil from the plastic dish. *The woman has died.* Those four words. The woman has died. Which woman? I asked, since the last time I'd checked everyone had seemed quite alive. The German woman, she said, the German woman in the wheelchair. She was meant to fly home today, her bag was packed and her coat on the chair, when she died.

Her impatient demands had finally been heard by the consulate, which arranged for her to be flown back to England on the next direct flight, but shortly before they came to fetch her one of her lungs collapsed and the other filled with water, too fast and too much to drain, and at 22:18 she crossed over into whatever underworld Germans inhabit, the nurse informed me. The next nurse who came in, this time to measure my temperature and pulse, elaborated further: they had all gone to see for themselves, they couldn't believe this had been the end of the feisty foreigner and her demands, forty minutes earlier she had been asking for a cup of coffee, no, not decaf, and then she took ill, so suddenly, had trouble drawing in breath, the doctors rushed her to intensive care but despite the fancy machines they lost her within minutes, and the nurse and her colleagues had lined up to watch her departure, pretending to be occupied with their clipboards when in reality all eyes were fixed on the corpse under the sheet, her lumpy outline like the silhouette of one of our volcanoes.

All that was left in her room was the strong smell of cigarette.

Three surgeries. Three rounds of anaesthesia. Each time I felt sawn in half and put back together differently. After the third round, of which I had scant recollection, the doctors closed the wound, convinced it was safe to do so. There seemed to be no lurking infection after all. With the terse nod of a policeman summoned on false alarm, the *infectólogo* bid me farewell while the nurse scribbled a few words in black marker on the clipboard. I could now go home, armed with a list of instructions and a final course of antibiotics.

Given the change in circumstances, I was relieved. Relieved not to have to face an empty corridor that night, or the following or the following. But I couldn't deny I felt abandoned. Doubly abandoned, actually, since not only had she taken such sudden leave but it turned out she had already been planning a departure, on more reasonable terms, of course, but a departure nevertheless, without saying goodbye. Would she have sent a nurse to fetch me, or left a note with her number, or simply left in silence? I would never know her intentions.

Back at home, it felt as though the cycles of life had been placed on fast-forward, and I wasn't the only creature adapting to change. In a cage in the kitchen trilled our one lone canary, whose song hadn't lost its joy despite the recent death of its partner, stiff-legged one morning beside the bowl of seeds. And then there was our ancient dog, even more ancient than when I'd left for hospital. Quiet, contrite, keeping to the corners, his wistful eyes turned in our direction whenever he heard his name. A few days ago he had been neutered and was adapting to life with a diminished drive. Over the past year or two his hind legs had grown weak and he climbed the stairs one by one, often pausing mid journey as if debating whether the summit was worth the effort. Now he'd lost further strength. I studied him from a distance, his clouded eyes and grizzled snout, resisting the urge to pet him since I now felt afraid. Animals in their twilight: one must forgive them. The unspoken thought in our house.

As for my hand, I couldn't bring myself to look at it though its form was obscured by endless loops of gauze. Heavy, unwieldy, more paw or mitt. Once a day my mother would tend to the dressing, an unusual moment of intimacy, and something like affection arose between us during those minutes when she unwrapped and dabbed and rewrapped while I turned away.

My forsaken hand, reduced without its companion. Activities in which I rarely partook were now off-limits and therefore more attractive. Clapping, praying, knitting. Others, such as the simple act of reading, felt like a gift: I'd hold down the book with my bandaged left and turn the pages with my dominant right. As the days went by, the doctor's instructions faded to a distant murmur. Use sling to sleep, and when leaving the house. When home, use hand as often as possible. Play the piano if there is one, type if you have a computer. Don't hold anything heavier than a cup of coffee. When I finally allowed myself to look I was unfazed by the sight, the skin around the stitches purple and swollen yet nothing as dramatic as the disfigurement I'd envisaged. Twice a day I washed it with warm water and liquid soap without ever submerging, and slowly, dutifully, it gathered strength.

However effortlessly, I looked after my hand far more carefully than my friend had looked after her lungs; after all, my hand simply had to be in repose whereas even in repose her lungs were at work, and I couldn't help dwelling on how much Wilhelmina had overexerted herself that final evening at her lantern. Yet the nurses were so rapt, no one had intervened, and perhaps we all only noticed her exhaustion after the show. Or had our nightly conversations and the circling draughts taken their toll? At moments these thoughts tormented me.

My remaining days in Mexico were spent in sloth mode. I seldom bothered getting dressed, having quickly fallen out of the habit. I knew it irritated my stepfather to see me in my pyjamas all day. If my mother protested I'd put on a sweater, one of my father's, for meals. I slept late, watched random things on television, attempted to play the piano (Bach, badly), and spent hours in the garden in the company of my mother's cacti collection in terracotta pots, taller and taller as they succumbed to the solar pull. After breakfast I'd lie on the grass in their shadow and read the paper, turning the pages gently so as not to disturb the hummingbirds that came to feed on the bougainvillea. I'd been so caught up in the hospital and Wilhelmina I'd forgotten the macabre stories unfolding in our country. I skimmed the headlines, avoided the details.

I had just dozed off in the garden, fresh air a blessing after so many days enclosed, when my mother stuck out her head and announced there was a phone call. It was one of the doctors – Wilhelmina's son was asking for our home number. Would it be fine to give it to him? There was no question. Any continuation of her existence would be a gift. The hours I then waited for him to call were filled with speculation: what was he calling about, would his voice be like hers, would he be haughty or polite?

I perched by the phone until it rang.

A young man asked for me.

This is Flora, I said.

Hi, this is Wilhelmina's son, Max. I believe you met my mother at the hospital.

I'm very sorry for your loss.

He mumbled a formality, acknowledging my condolences, and then: I have a request and hope it's not too odd . . . My mother left a bag. They're shipping her suitcase but I would really like her bag to be brought in person. If I'm not mistaken, you live in London too. I'm pretty sure that's what my mother said. Would you mind . . . ?

It was more than a little thrilling to imagine Wilhelmina mentioning me to her son, my existence made known to a stranger across the ocean. But I wondered whether to accept, reminded of the friend who feared the *pez diablo* might be hexed. Yes, that's fine, I said, deciding to check the contents before travel.

I can't tell you how much I appreciate it . . . She would have too.

After jotting down various details I told him I'd be in touch. Thank you again, he said, and in the meantime he'd arrange for the bag to be delivered. His accent was much more British than his mother's but laced with hints of elsewhere, and I couldn't help wondering, as he spoke, what sort of person was attached to the voice. In my experience, you can never trust portraits painted by parents.

Two afternoons later, a taxi driver brought by a black leather bag with red handles, as capacious as the ones doctors used to carry in the past. I let it sit for a day, getting used to its presence, before looking inside. An overpowering smell of stale tobacco wafted out as I unzipped the top and pulled the sides wide apart to examine the contents: a notebook, a set of keys on a silver ankh keychain, four ballpoint pens, a purple change purse, an unopened bag of liquorice cats, a pair of glasses in a felt pouch, two paper clips, a marbled stone with smooth edges, a dark blue button, a handful of business cards of antique dealers in Mexican cities and European towns, an unused ticket for the Mexico City metro, an adaptor plug, and a strip of paracetamol with four missing tablets. At the bottom of the bag sat the lantern in its cardboard box. There was also a box of slides, pressed tightly together. I opened the notebook. Angular scrawls in German, slanted lances and towers like the handwriting of a medieval queen.

On my last afternoon in Mexico the phone rang again. I could tell it was the son from the way my mother cupped the receiver, an intermediary in a highly confidential operation. This time he was calling with a thornier question. Would I bring his mother's ashes, he asked. Your mother's ashes? I repeated. Yes, the matter had been taken care of and someone at the consulate had done the paperwork and they just needed an individual to transport them. He wouldn't have asked me to fly out with a body but these were just ashes in a temporary urn, really not heavy at all, he said, as though that were the issue. It would be such an enormous favour, he added. I felt like saying this was not what I had signed up for. I'd expected to return to London with a new friendship, not a reliquary. But I accepted. My mother agreed I should say yes; my stepfather said it was an imposition, a favour too far. In the middle of dinner the same taxi driver, an elderly man with a white moustache, brought over the remains of my hospital companion in a black velvet bag. Judging from his jovial manner he had no idea what he had just delivered.

Appetite gone, I excused myself and hurried up to my room. Inside the velvet bag was a plastic liner bag and, in that, a sealed cardboard box with a label.

Name of deceased: Wilhelmina Blau
Date of Birth: 04/03/1945
Sex: Female
Relative/contact information: Max Blau

On the morning of my trip I took a break from packing, my suitcase never fully unpacked, and went in search of Diogenes. I found him under the dining-room table. His eyes met mine but he didn't shift position. I crept over to where he lay between the table legs, taking in the clouded landscape of his cataracts and the grizzled snout with missing whiskers. Old age had claimed him. And it was old age that had bitten me. I stroked his head with my good hand, murmured a few words in our language reserved for animals, and with those motions something was laid to rest.

Look after your hand, my stepfather said, make sure nothing happens to it back in London, that's all we need, for you to want help and none of your vagabond friends to have time the way your mother has had this past month. Look after your hand, he repeated as we said goodbye outside the airport terminal, my mother waving from the car.

The weather at departure is stormy, the weather at our destination is stormy, and we wish you a very good flight, the captain was to announce two hours later as I sat strapped into my seat looking out at the strip of blue lights lining the runway. Our plane began to taxi. Travelling at night never failed to produce an overwhelming emptiness, the sense I had no home, no roots, anywhere, that I existed in a perpetual limbo, everywhere and nowhere, never somewhere. I skipped dinner but ate the bag of liquorice cats and drank a Bloody Mary with my temazepam and then wrapped myself in the flimsy airplane blanket, with Wilhelmina's bag and ashes in the overhead compartment.

II

Magic. Lantern. Whenever I look back and ask myself how my life intersected with this seemingly archaic device, how an instrument I knew nothing about appeared one day to flaunt its bygone power, I'm still surprised by the circuitous trajectory, particularly of an object so steady in aim. And what if a person can be like that lantern, casting images, illuminating corners, still very present long after they've gone?

My father, who worked in electricity, would have probably been sceptical. He had always been obsessed with the latest technology and did not look back in time. He knew all about light bulbs, and the filament's many shapes. He preferred distributed light, a democratic, uniform supply, to the concentrated one of any primeval fire. And he was much more interested in turning night into day than day into night. Upon coming home from work he would switch on every light in the house. After he vanished a cousin assured me he hadn't left entirely, that he would continue speaking to me through electricity, every flicker a message. I waited and waited. No signs ever came. A flickering light was only that, a flickering light, the death throes of a bulb in need of replacing.

A year before he left us, my father returned one evening in a dark mood. He trudged past us and up to his room. Still in his jacket, he fell onto the bed and told us that someone at work had been electrocuted. They were all aware of electricity's two-faced gift; every now and then, electricity herself would remind them. The man had worked at the company for twelve years. My father had been responsible for his assignment that day, sending him to repair some street cables after a recent storm. My mother told him it wasn't his fault, how could he have known, and began to utter a few commonplaces about the hereafter. He interrupted. *Aquí se acaba*. It ends here. At the funeral a week later a long procession of electricians from the Sindicato Mexicano de Electricistas paraded down Reforma clutching fiery orange and purple wreaths which they later deposited on the newly dug grave at the Panteón de Dolores. That night, the flowers were stolen by street children who sold them at traffic lights the following day. *Aquí se acaba*. I too did not believe in an afterlife. Nor in any kind of magic. And yet every so often, a door would open or close on its own.

I'd had to change planes in Madrid and then wait five hours for my connecting flight, performing complex balancing acts with my luggage with the help of my one strong hand. It was past midnight by the time I reached home, the sight of the house, its facade partially lit by the street lamps, more welcome than ever. My landlords had long gone to bed. The usual lights had been left on in the hallway and the landing. Keeping their distance the cats followed me up the stairs, wary yet intrigued by the foreign scents emanating from my suitcase. Lurker and his sister Pouncer. Inscrutable witnesses to my life and I to much of theirs. Yet I'd given them scant thought while away. Here they were again, greeting me from afar, testing the waters before our dialogue resumed. Lurker was the more timid of the two, always observing from a distance, leaving Pouncer to act out their joint desires. Sedentary by day, they'd often fight at night, a release of all that coiled energy. Both weighed over six kilos, I'd rarely seen such hefty cats, every jump onto a surface or return to the floor accompanied by a loud thud. Sometimes one of them would chase the other to the top of the stairs and there outside my door they would conduct their gigantomachy. My landlords claimed to hear nothing but I'd be kept awake by the caterwauls, worried they were drowning out something terrible, like an assassination while the band is playing.

Top floors should create a sense of freedom, a welcome unshackling from the more terrestrial floors below, but that was never the case for mine. My three top rooms were tranquil, neutral and intermittently tidy but my mind never felt ordered within them. I spent many hours alone in the house – my landlords were often away, prey to a zeal for travel once in possession of their pensioners' passes – but I rarely ventured downstairs in their absence. *Quiet lodger* they'd put in their listing, a quiet lodger to feed the cats and keep the top floor alive. The tenant before me, a burlesque dancer in her twenties, hadn't lasted more than a year. I suspect they added 'quiet' to the listing after she left. Now and then I'd come across a trace of her, a red feather shed by a boa or a few glinting sequins under the bed, not to mention the lingering smell of varnish in the bathroom, where she must have painted her nails as she dolled herself up for the night. A number of spiders joined me in those top rooms, some of alarming girth and others so wispy I was never sure whether they were alive or had gradually faded to ghosts in their webs. I wondered what had transpired in the spider kingdom while I was away.

I lay down in my clothes, too weary to change out of them, or perhaps reluctant to shed the layers I'd slipped on in Mexico the previous day, aware of a profound hope I'd been nourishing: that the apathy and inertia I'd been battling before my trip had been shaken off. That something – shape, form, tone, to be determined – had come to take their place. Throughout the hospital stay I'd welcomed every development as a sign of imminent change, I didn't want to let go of any of it, could not allow it to vanish after my return. Usually something atrophies during a stay in hospital but in my case, I couldn't help feeling, something had been activated.

Weeks felt like months. From my bed I surveyed my room for traces of occupation. You never know what landlords get up to while you're away. A shirtsleeve hung out of the hamper like a person drowning in dirty laundry. Curtains, two-thirds drawn. A blunt pencil on the desk, the sharpener stuffed with shavings. Had it been me who had worn that shirt, drawn the curtains, written with that pencil?

That's the worst dog bite I've ever seen but it's been beautifully sewn up, said my GP as he studied the front and the palm. Twelve days after the final surgery, the swelling had subsided and the extraction could begin. I took a deep breath and tried to summon picturesque thoughts as one by one he pulled out the stitches.

The son and I had yet to agree on a day for me to deliver his mother's things. And not only her things, of course, but his mother in another form. I had work, he was caught up in matters undisclosed, or was perhaps putting off the moment. Wilhelmina's bag, ashes and lantern continued to sit in my closet, where I'd stored them after my return. One night I caved in to curiosity and unwrapped the lantern and set it on the table. It had little tin claws with knuckles. And slats on either side, almost like gills, on the base and chimney top. It really wasn't that large, and in my mind had grown even smaller since Wilhelmina's show. A tin plaque attached to its forehead contained a tower, flanked by the initials JF, in an oval frame. Below them, in a scroll, were the words MADE IN GERMANY. There was a door at the back, like a steam engine's boiler room, which you could tug open. Walled inside was a bulb: the light source. At some stage the original wick, probably capable of setting a home on fire, had been replaced. On the inside of the lid, a sheet with instructions.

I'd imagined what it would be like to bring it out, yes, we would have held staring contests across the room, the lantern and I, each time I would have been the one to eventually look away, and in the insomnia of unfinished conversations I would have conducted my own. You see, the thing is, I would say, the woman has died. Yes, *that* woman. And that's why you are here with me and not with her. You are here with me in these top rooms, in this house where I hope not to live for much longer, because as you know situations can carry on for ages if you're not careful. Or they can change in an instant.

There it sat, no more animated than any of the other objects in the room, yet I could feel the old resistance creeping back, a resistance to anything that smacked even vaguely of the fantastic, anything that even vaguely departed from the real. But this wasn't magic, I told myself, it was illusion. And I couldn't help feeling I should bring it to life, just once, plug it in and see what happened when I introduced a current. I should try it out, shouldn't I, before returning it to the son. In Japan they say that tools and utensils turn into monsters if neglected for too long. If neglected for a century, actually, but surely objects behave differently in every country.

> *Directions for the use of a magic lantern*
>
> 1. *Place the magic lantern on a table so that the lens is facing a white wall at a distance of 1–1.5 metres.*
>
> 2. *Carefully clean lens, remove any dust from the metallic mirror, and fill the lamp reservoir with oil. Trim the wick. A clear, steady image requires a bright flame.*

3. *Now insert the slides upside down into the lantern so that the images appear right side up. Move the focusing tube in or out until the picture is sharp.*

4. *The further the table is from the wall, the larger but less distinct the images will appear. The closer, the smaller, the sharper.*

5. *The most splendid effect is produced if the room is entirely dark. Always check for light spills.*

I lifted the lantern out of its box, plugged it in, and pointed its lens towards an empty patch of wall. I closed the curtains and switched it on. A glowing circle of light was cast, a hungry circle waiting to see what sorts of beings might come to fill the vacancy.

Let me see, let me see, everyone cried out on my first day back at work. I held out my hand as they crowded round, and pointed out the places where the dog had bitten me. Once their curiosity had been satisfied, or probably secretly let down, we all returned to our bays. Had anyone missed me? I searched for telltale signs as Paul, our main designer, approached with a mug of tea. He held it out towards my left hand and I guessed his intention. To test my grip. I accepted the mug with my right.

The first time I'd descended into our dimly lit workshop, tenebrosity a part of our work ethic and aesthetic, I felt I'd entered a giant's cavernous interior, or that of a biblical whale. A whale or a giant with an appetite for silver. At our bays we each had a lamp, boosted by strips of overhead lighting. Yet we preferred to work penumbrally, and would switch off the overhead illumination the moment our manager left the premises. We were all elves down there, hammering and polishing in the semi-darkness, attuned to the sound of silver in our hands and the occasional footstep overhead.

If something scratches your hand as you turn it over, you know where the snag lies. Imperfections in silver are easier to locate via touch than sight and I prided myself on quickly locating any. After one of our jewellers left it was decided, I never knew on what basis, that I was best qualified to take over assessment for repairs. Once a week a tray of imperfect objects would be placed before me: a precious stone that'd fallen out and needed to be reglued, a broken clasp or link, a ring that was too tight or too loose for a finger. This last would be a gift, usually, although I was always surprised by how often customers got the sizing wrong for their own hands. We do not know our own hands.

At work I was the only person who moved between floors, back and forth between the till and the buffing machine (my fellow polisher, whose calico mops frequently spun at full speed), and as if to spell out this distinction my bay had a table that could be raised and lowered with a crank, up to waist level when I wished to stand and lowered when I wanted to return to sitting. My colleagues coveted my protean table and the emergency button under my foot, there to stop the flight of any spindles that came loose. You could indulge whatever thoughts you had, angry, nasty, eldritch thoughts you would never share with anyone, but the instrument you wielded while having those thoughts had to be kept under control. Otherwise it could, at any moment, spell your undoing.

Unlike the rest of us Paul was untrained, his talent shaped entirely by instinct and things glimpsed in movies and magazines. His great-grandfather had been a shipbuilder in the London docks and he himself had come from a job in manufacturing at the Ford assembly line in Dagenham, where in his free time he would craft trinkets out of spare parts. Word spread about how skilled he was with his hands, and before long he was selling things here and there. After factory closures, each more brutal than the last, he found himself out of job and flat and was sleeping on his brother's sofa. One night at a club a friend was wearing a ring Paul had fashioned out of a metal bolt and this ring caught the attention of our founding jeweller, who contacted him the following day. Paul's hair was cropped short when he'd begun working here but had been left to grow to biker length, falling around his shoulders when released from its bun. Only he could read my moods, the tenor of the thoughts I fed into my machine, and I felt his eyes on me as I reached for a black bristle brush.

In Spanish to '*dar vueltas*' to a situation means to turn it over in your mind. The same thing occurs when I turn the silver in my hand. I am holding a thought, seeking the best angle from which to approach it, just long enough to give it the right amount of shine. That's when I do my best thinking, while polishing the silver, especially when hardly anyone is talking and the air is filled with hammering, sanding and soldering, sounds that ease the passage between thoughts. The shop upstairs, however, is governed by music, from the moment we open until the moment we roll down the shutters, and the only genre we all agree on is heavy metal, the tempo and temper best matched to our skull rings. Whenever we crave a bit more verve down below we wire our speakers to the shop stereo and nurture a spiritual connection to the industrial towns in the north of England where, Paul likes to remind us, many heavy metal bands originated, inspired by all the loud clanging and machinery.

One afternoon as 'The Unforgiven' was starting to play, our shop was visited by a handsome stranger. I'd never known what this Metallica song was about yet felt certain this man had stepped out of it. He may have been a musician. Every few months a famous musician would appear in search of an eloquent ring, often a skull. *A ring with presence, real presence, something fans will notice from afar.*

I'd therefore seen many a rock star but could rarely identify them, only sensed they were famous by the way they went about the shop spreading their aura. Heavy metal threw me into a state of longing, which meant I spent most of my hours upstairs in its grip. The throbbing music always made me want more from life, made me want to up the ante in nearly every situation, and now the combination of a favourite Metallica song and this handsome stranger was almost too much. Too much for my galloping heart, which would have probably burst and splattered its contents all over the display cabinets had a caveat not suddenly brought things to a halt: his jacket, I now noticed, had a bushy fur trim. It was a serious problem as the days turned colder, this proliferation of fur trims, reminders of all the plundered fields and woodlands, and the chillier the air grew, the more fur that came into sight like animals risen from the dead. Even from a distance I could distinguish between fake fur and stolen, fur stolen from an animal had a particular bounce to it and the hairs parted in the breeze, reminding you of the life that once animated it, whereas fake fur had a synthetic gloss and didn't shift so much in the wind. It was just as well that Paul was off sick that day, since apart from being a master jeweller he was a Hunt Saboteur, and in his world every fur trim represented a defeat.

Yes, this man with the fur trim was impossibly handsome, in fact the most handsome person I had seen in years. But I couldn't help suspecting he had traded something in, perhaps his own heart, for all that beauty. The jet-black hair, the translucent skin, the dramatic cheekbones and the icy blue eyes must have come at a price. All of a sudden he caught me staring. I quickly moved my gaze to the jacket, noting the type of fur: coyote. Normally I would ask whether I could be of assistance but I was too inhibited by his looks, too wound up over the trim. He had now paused at the skulls, as if to commune with a few ancestors – wrapped around his left little finger, I saw, was our Smallest Evil Skull ring – and leaned over the display cabinet, bringing his face to the glass. His jacket seemed to get in the way. He removed it and tucked it under an arm. Despite the autumn chill he was wearing nothing but a cotton T-shirt, and his neck, arms and hands were tattooed with runic symbols. There were too many, and too close together, to decipher. And furthermore, I wouldn't have had time; after a few moments, perhaps unnerved by my staring, he slipped on his jacket and left in the same icy silence, just as the song was fading out.

Even with Wilhelmina's ashes and lantern in the room I was, to my surprise, sleeping better than I had in years. Despite the mental churning and unsettling additions I would lie down at night and wake up eight hours later in almost the exact same position, the covers hardly creased. At first I thought it was the result of the powerful potions the doctors had given me, or the aftermath of three rounds of anaesthesia. A prolonged spell of jet lag. Domestic rhythms, and a welcome reunion with my bed. But several weeks on, I had to accept the fact: somehow, I had been returned to the world a better sleeper. I could only conclude that during my stay in hospital my inner clock had been reset, but was hesitant to cry victory too soon.

The son and I finally agreed on a date. That Sunday I wrapped the lantern in a cloth and laid it in its box, then in the bag. I carried the heavier bag in my right hand, the ashes in my left. As the contents rattled about I wondered what sort of person I was going to meet, whether he would be half as formidable as his mother, and thought back on a family trip many years ago to Sanlúcar de Barrameda, an Andalusian town, to visit some distant cousins. On our second day we'd gone on a tour of a *manzanilla* warehouse where the dry sherry of the region was distilled. A young man with glasses led us through its cavernous rooms, casks stacked high under the stone arches. *FINO, OLOROSO, AMONTILLADO PRINCIPE, MOSCATEL ECO* read the names painted onto the casks in ghostly white letters. The principal warehouse, La Catedral, was built in such a way that different winds blew in from every axis helping to ripen the *manzanilla*, the wind from the Levant, for instance, adding a salty note to the barrels it swept past. Our tour ended with a tasting in a room upstairs, four types of sherry ranging from the very dry to the sensually sweet – I was only fourteen, and imbibing spirits for the first time – and as we sipped from the spindly glasses our guide told us how every drop contained residue of the Mother from one hundred years ago, the way fermented things like sourdough also bore a trace of *la masa madre*. Years later I still remembered one line: 'Cada gota contiene su madre.' Every drop contains its mother.

I boarded the 73 bus and jostled my way to the back, only to discover an inkblot on the afternoon: an enormous Rottweiler, his four enormous paws straddling two seats. A scruffy man gripping a dented can of Carlsberg was his companion, his own feet propped on the seat in front of him. I tried to backtrack but the passengers behind me were pressing me forward and soon I was only a foot away from the pair. You mustn't be scared of dogs from now on, had been my doctor's parting words, well, now we were all being put to the test, not only passengers with bitten hands, and I tried to recall what the surgeon had said about a Rottweiler's bite force, whether it was above or below that of an Alsatian, and though this particular dog had quite an amiable expression, in fact more amiable than most of the humans around him, I alighted at the next stop and walked the rest of the way.

The autumn sun had yet to withdraw and along the canal there was a fair amount of activity among its residents. A man with hair streaked blue and green rolled himself a cigarette aboard *Susie Two*. A couple of women were busy strapping a wheelbarrow to the roof of their floating home while a mottled pigeon, an entire cloudscape on its wing, pecked at something nearby. A ginger cat sat in a window surrounded by peeling paint: the boat's wary eye looking left, looking right, as the animal changed position, alert in the ageing vessel. *My son, he's a bit adrift*, Wilhelmina had said, but anchor and drift must surely be relative if you live amid houseboats.

The house sat right alongside the canal. Sleepwalk out of bed and you would end up in the water. Cross its surface and you would enter a boat. I was only a few minutes late but there he was, standing in the doorway as though he'd been waiting and waiting for me to arrive. Eyes and mouth a bit too large for his face, or perhaps he had lost so much weight that certain features had receded and others come to the fore. Thick curly hair brushed to the side, protesting. My first impression was of a shy nocturnal mammal, more hedgehog than pangolin, in grey trousers, black turtleneck and striped socks. There he stood, at the threshold, reluctantly. As if not wanting to be seen. But he had no choice. We had made an appointment.

He waved as I approached, his face slowly coming into focus. Max, he mumbled, though I of course knew his name. Flora, I said, though he knew mine too. How attached are you to your shoes? was the first question he ever asked me. For a few moments I was confused, had he mistaken me for the tragic ballerina of a film, until noticing the heap – loafers, brogues, sandals and other footwear – at the entrance. It must have been one of his mother's house rules. I knelt down to unlace my boots and left them beside a pair of Birkenstocks, then followed him down a corridor with mirrors and grandfather clocks. Impossible to ignore your face, or time, if you turned.

The living room had wide windows with vertical grilles that gave onto the canal. Tasselled lamps stood in every corner (no overhead light) and at every wall a bookshelf, where figurines outnumbered the books. Two armchairs, upholstered in a dark green fabric with purple comets, dominated the space, along with a flat-screen television that emitted a low hum. A cane lay propped against a cupboard. Everything seemed to be on standby. I handed Max his mother's bag, a twinge of remorse as I let go of the handles, and then the ashes. The men and women at Mexico City airport security had been intrigued by the magic lantern, I told him, and asked me to open the box after it passed through the X-ray machine. As for the ashes, they didn't feel the need to investigate after glancing at the paperwork. I studied his face, searching for familiar features in the long nose, crooked teeth, puckish ears. Attractive, at an angle.

Before examining the bag he went to the window and looked out at the canal, then moved on to me as though to relay its message, which was to enquire, with surprising detachment, after his mother's last days. I told him about the first time I'd seen her, a mysterious figure at the end of the corridor, that's all she'd been at first, and explained how the nurse had waved me over and asked me to translate, and Wilhelmina's incessant request for a cigarette, and yes, she'd mentioned she had a son, whom she didn't want to leave alone for too long, and, once, a husband. I told him about the pumps of gel and the stretch of corridor with the hissing light and the nurses in green, for the most part obliging. I omitted his mother's great appetite, the sort of metaphysical hunger that sometimes sweeps over people who are approaching death, although I would never know whether she'd sensed the end was near. And, lastly, I told him about the magic lantern show she put on in her room but did not mention, since how could I be sure, that this exertion may have been her undoing.

Have a seat, he said, as he settled into an armchair.

He picked up the bag and the sack.

Funny, I thought these would weigh more.

What, the ashes?

He didn't reply.

Here I was, in her home, face-to-face with her son, inhaling traces of her cigarettes, the scent of which still hung over everything. If something like two per cent of the air we breathe was breathed by dinosaurs how much of this air would have passed through Wilhelmina? It's easy to romanticise the dead, especially when through wild circumstance you end up forming part of their final days, more than the people they were close to in life.

I remember when she was packing for her trip, he said, debating until the night before whether to undertake such a lengthy journey. But she'd always wanted to go to Mexico and knew it was her only chance.

Bag on lap like a long-lost Pekinese, he told me about the last day they'd spent together. Wilhelmina had dragged him to a matinee at the Curzon. A Czech film, from the seventies. She needed to relax before the flight. The only others in the cinema were an old woman and a man in a bulky, architectural hat. They arrived twenty minutes late but no matter, it was still the opening scene: a soldier in an empty lot watching a crow grooming its feathers on a leafless tree. At first he couldn't tell whether it was meant to be in colour or black and white, everything was so monochrome, but then someone appeared wearing a yellow scarf. His mother told him to nap if he was bored, which he was. Yet she was quickly drawn into the sluggish melancholy of the film, one of those ponderous films structured around silence and minutiae (her words), and she stepped out to smoke only once. When he woke up from his nap he began to fixate on the hat diagonally across from them, it wasn't blocking their view but he felt it absorbing all of the energy in the space, the way bushy beards often do, and it began to give him a headache. After a while the old lady walked out and then, twenty minutes later, the hat. Eventually his mother had one of her hunger attacks so they went to Pizza Express, leaving the film to play to an empty theatre. That night she packed for her trip while he rested in his room with a bag of frozen peas on his forehead and the next morning she knocked on his door to say goodbye. He still felt guilty for not helping with her suitcase.

This was the longest he'd spoken. He had such a guarded air. A small house at the end of an overgrown garden.

I heard the sound of spinning, elsewhere in the room. That's Isidore, he said, as I tried to locate the noise. Isidore? Our mouse.

Had Wilhelmina ever mentioned a mouse? Perhaps in passing, an outlandish detail swept up in a wider conversation, but I was surprised I'd missed it. Max gestured towards a tank sitting on a table in a corner of the room. The mouse leapt off its wheel when it saw me approach. It came to the glass. Pale grey fur, petal ears, shiny intelligent eyes. I stared down and the mouse stared up.

Max was now looking towards the windows. Towards but not through them, I sensed, at something not there. After all, it'd been less than a month. Did he prefer to be alone or did he welcome company? Best to err on the side of discretion. I should go now, I said, and began buttoning my coat. He didn't protest, only said there was something he wanted me to take, otherwise he would have to toss it into the canal. Something that'd been in his mother's suitcase. He opened a drawer and handed me an object wrapped in Mexican newspaper. Take this hideous thing, he said. Through the wrapping I could feel the *pez diablo*'s jagged skeleton.

He thanked me for bringing what I brought. I again offered my condolences. It must be very strange for your mother to go on a trip and never return.

Yes, he said, yes.

The sky had turned a marbled black and dusk silenced the canal. Apart from the occasional shadow or bicycle on the move, the path lay empty and the boat people had retreated into their homes, the portholes like faint bobbing moons. With most visual coordinates removed my other senses were thrown into relief, and for the first time ever I heard the creaking of tethered boats, the thick ropes tightening with the current and then relaxing, a constant tug and repose, as they were pushed off and pulled back to the bank.

In our workshop, a procession of silver skulls traced a path between the things we yearned for in life and the hereafter. There was another image, too. On the wall directly above where I sat hung a postcard of a William Blake engraving, *I want! I want!* The owner of the shop had taped it there over a decade ago before dying of a heart attack at sixty-three, having attained much of what he'd dreamt of, presumably, but his two children, the heirs, lived in Goa and rarely came by, leaving the business in the hands of a taciturn executor with an aversion to silver. From my bay I'd study the postcard and wonder what emotions the scene had conjured up in the owner. Against a cross-hatched sky dotted with seven erratic stars, a curious figure full of yearning stands at the base of a tall ladder leading up to the moon, one foot already on a rung. The figure wears an oval shield over its face, almost like a fencer's mask or an early space helmet. Watching from nearby are two other figures: the woman extends an arm towards the climber, the man seems to be holding her back. Don't be fooled by dreams, he might be saying. But the yearning figure is driven and determined and has begun his ascent. Not for him, this terrestrial solitude.

Seeing as you were her last friend, is what Max had said as I knelt down to lace up my boots, you should come to my mother's memorial, next Saturday noon at the Ragged School Museum. Nothing religious, just a place where she put on a few shows. *Her last friend.* Those were his words. Had she called me a friend or was it simply his assumption? We were on the path to friendship, it had felt that way, albeit a path forged by her stories, not mine, and I would never know whether the friendship would have continued in London and, if so, in what form. It would have surely lessened in intensity, each of us pulled back into the demands of our daily lives, no longer confined to a hospital corridor abroad. And what about the son? An unfinished portrait, in fact only just begun.

Before going to the memorial I read about the Ragged School in Mile End, a row of brick warehouses on the canal at Copperfield Road that Dr Thomas Barnardo, one of the most inspired philanthropists of the Victorian era, had converted into a school for destitute children in 1877. Food was provided, and clothing too. Boys and girls with factory jobs took evening classes. The numbers grew rapidly, and before long it became the largest ragged school in London. Tens of thousands of impoverished children, the sons and daughters of hawkers, knife grinders, costermongers and wandering showmen, passed through its doors. Most lived in Limehouse Fields, a poor, crowded district on the other side of the canal. I couldn't help imagining a ragged school as an asymmetrical building with jagged edges, but this one was long and stately and anything but that (the name referred to the children's tattered clothes).

The pediment was visible from a distance, the bell in the tympanum at a permanent tilt. Beyond the green metal doors an eccentric mix was already gathering at the entrance, nearly everyone in Victorian black with accents of purple via a scarf, ribbon or tie. Many generations seemed present: apart from the faces, it could be seen in the hat or the stride. I felt too shy to mingle and Max was nowhere in sight. There was still half an hour; I decided to explore the building to see whether I could guess the space where Wilhelmina might have put on her shows.

It wasn't difficult to envision the crates and machinery once stored within the high ceilings and pocked turquoise walls. At some of the bays, warehouse cranes emerged like claws or peered in from outside like expectant birds. Fed, now waiting to enter. A green wheelbarrow. An old printing press. Rusted loading carts. An upturned platform on wheels. A short wooden ladder. Abandoned faucets. Scenic islands of exposed brick. Articulate beams, some still with pulley. And forgotten bolts, painted over many times, that seemed to hold the building together. The light from outside, assisted by the intervening geometry of the window frames, created a beautiful effect on nearly every surface. In the attic they'd recreated the spartan home of a Victorian hairbrush-maker, everything but the pillow and crockery given a dusting of soot. On the table, as if handled a moment ago, lay a deconstructed hairbrush. The room opposite contained an assembly of chairs, cabinets and boxes, and two crestfallen mannequins in a corner. A row of clunky old sewing machines sat on a shelf – after the school closed, the building was occupied by different rag merchants who made popular men's suits and distinctive leather jackets. And beyond the shelf of sewing machines, between a three-legged table and a decrepit stove called Britannia, was an empty patch of wall. I decided this would have been where Wilhelmina rearranged the furniture, blacked out the windows and set up her lantern.

The memorial was to be held in a classroom on the first floor, the door propped open with a metal doorstopper in the shape of a spiral. There was a fireplace, and six rows of wooden desks, each one attached to a bench by a heavy cast-iron frame. Most of the desks were already occupied by mourners who chatted among themselves as they waited for the service to begin. At the front of the room stood a crooked abacus and a blackboard covered in simple mathematical equations. I felt myself shrinking to child size as I sat down at one of the few free desks, across from a white-haired couple in silky waistcoats, and raised the lid to peer inside. Four stumps of chalk, a thin rag, a slate writing board. I let the lid fall just as a man with a walking stick came to sit beside me in a blast of patchouli. I moved aside a little and then glanced around the room. There was Max, by the entrance. Arms crossed, leaning against the wall, in a blue Adidas tracksuit. As though he had just come in from a run. He was the only person standing. I waved but he didn't wave back and I couldn't tell whether he'd seen me. On a cabinet sat a framed portrait of his mother beside a dunce cap no one thought of removing. It was an odd choice of photograph: in it, she was turning away from the camera, as if someone were calling her name.

And then one by one, as though summoned by a figure of authority who'd wielded power in the space long ago, people from Wilhelmina's life walked up to the front. They took their places between the blackboard and the abacus but instead of adding insight into historical measurements and equations they provided their name, a brief description of their relationship to the deceased, and their testimony, voices timid at first but building in confidence. Some were brief, others unfurled into detail, some read from a paper, others spoke more freely, and from my desk I listened closely as memory upon memory filled the draughty room, and the more they spoke and the more I listened the more the faces and voices merged into one vast portrait, everything transforming or dissolving into something else, no scene, no existence, ever self-contained.

You would apprehend the smell and the person at once. Even with her back to the door you'd know when Wilhelmina had entered the pub. She would light one cigarette on the back of the last, rarely a pause between, and had the skin and the breathing of someone who didn't see much of the sun. Her movements were slow, she was in her seventies as you know, but her eyes were as quick as a taxi meter. She'd complain that English trains and speed limits were lessons in patience.

Wilhelmina was that rare thing, a female collector. And that made her tougher than any man. A chimney stack against the wind. She knew the value of everything. And was never taken for a fool. Once at a fair she had a showdown with a collector over a daguerreotype, the man had a personal attachment whereas for Wilhelmina it was simply an object that struck her fancy, and she stared him down until the man stormed off. If she spotted something she wanted nothing could stand in her way, and certainly not the will of another collector. She didn't like to league with anyone, she ran her own show, and hated to compromise.

Her mind pretty much contained the knowledge of her library and she would supplement each illusion with scholarship. Everything in her home was shadowed by scholarship, there wasn't a single blank page, she didn't believe in blank pages and would prefer if the world held none. Lunar topography, Renaissance anatomy, Athanasius Kircher – she could talk about anything, for hours.

Oh she could be bossy, couldn't she? I loved Wilhelmina but it wasn't always easy to spend time with her, I imagine many of you would agree. She lived right near our boat on the canal. We would drop by her house for a cuppa or she would come to us, especially in autumn, when she liked to be near the water and watch the ducks fussing about their nests. But she could be bossy, and tell us how we'd got the furniture wrong, how we should move this and that. One day she just picked up the heavy bench by the window and dragged it to another spot. It's still there.

She hated the thought of people not paying attention. Hers was the language of a showman, scholar or magician – well, wasn't she all three? – and when asked a question she'd pause and say, What do YOU think?, turning things around to check how closely you were listening. She loved to bring out her perspective box of the Earthquake of Lisbon, I think it was built in Augsburg in the 1780s, and show you this cardboard recreation of the disaster that shook not only Portugal but all of Enlightenment thought. The box had seven layers showing collapsed buildings and figures strewn about. There was one arm emerging from the rubble, twisting upwards, and she'd ask whether you could spot it.

She emailed us daily about her exhibition here in London, but then got carried away and sent too many boxes and the gallery had to return half. Not to mention everything reeked of tobacco when we opened it. That wasn't all. The wiring in some instruments was very old. So old, in fact, that our in-house technician kept getting electrical shocks while installing, especially the peep show with the turning crank. Pete got a massive shock from it and said this had been the hardest exhibition he had ever worked on.

At university in the sixties Wilhelmina was involved in anti-war and anti-nuclear protests. In those days, there was one a month. First protests, then conventions. After Jan died she went to as many magic lantern conventions as she could. And I went with her since she didn't like to go alone. At one in Ghent, people watched as she finished off her sherry outside a bar and tossed the glass into the back of her battered blue station wagon, where it sank into the travelling jumble. Every so often, she would say that the value of her collection was that it held the grammar of everything that is possible. When she parted with it, she parted with that sense of possibility.

It's true she was intimidating, even truculent at times, but she was also generous and kind, and had that youthful habit of flicking the hair off her face with her hand. She did this so often in fact that once a visiting politician waved back at her through the window of a cafe, thinking she was greeting him as he walked past.

Many words have been said about Wilhelmina the collector, but what about Wilhelmina the performer? She was so elegant at the lantern. Would transform. At the Geographical Society, she projected a series of natural disasters, entire landscapes destroyed just like that. And she loved dissolving views, one scene slowly eclipsed by another: summer by autumn, night deepening around the ruins of a chateau, the Brocken spectre over a mountaintop. At the Natural History Museum, she cast nineteenth-century French slides of insects. At an AA meeting, temperance slides from the 1870s. At the top of a sex shop in Soho, a series of Victorian pornography. Wilhelmina would speak very little during her spectacle. She was as you might suspect a purist that way, wanted the images to be the centre of attention. She would let each one begin in silence, allowing expectation to build, and only then say a few words. Not often but occasionally she'd wear period dress, and always arrived early to check the space for light spills (you could never trust others to do so). After the shows people would gather round her instrument, full of questions. She once said it was important to rein in the banter, too much chipped away at the mystery, but too little might fail to launch the image. And to seat sceptics at the back, the susceptible at the front, and the curious and agnostic in the middle. But then she stopped putting on shows, didn't she, and went to work at the Warburg.

What would I have said had I been invited to speak? My memories were limited, they had no history, no time to evolve, but they would have been the final ones. Her appetite, her requests, her acts of reminiscence: I would have spoken about all three. Was my version of the person that different from the versions I had just heard? Perhaps not, and yet as I listened I couldn't help feeling she was *my* Wilhelmina, not theirs, I had seen her, known her, heard her, last. The nurses, the doctors and I: we were the final cast.

There would now be refreshments in the room below, visitors encouraged to donate what they could to the museum. I sensed movement at the back and turned to see Max stealing out, a figure in blue in the midst of vanishing. Well, he had already been erased from the picture. For the entire hour he had stood there, implicit in nearly every story, his name was never uttered. People manoeuvred themselves out from behind the tiny desks, returning to adults as they stretched their legs, released from the grasp of imaginary children. I jostled past them a bit unceremoniously and rushed down the wooden stairs towards the entrance. It was only four in the afternoon yet the sky had begun to darken. Shadows with heartbeats, precision relaxing its hold. Max was nowhere in sight.

As you grow older your fantasy life starts slipping away, early daydreams, romantic and professional, less and less likely to materialise. The options narrow, ships set sail one by one. I had seen many, many ships depart. In my mid-thirties the harbour, once crowded, had begun to empty. But what were my fantasies, exactly? Supple, malleable and open to fluctuation. Willing, to a degree, to adapt to a new person or situation, as long as said person or situation didn't reveal itself too entirely. But if I were truly honest, they were probably more monolithic. Perhaps the moment had come to forsake some of the fantasies and go off-piste.

After the memorial Max failed to reply to my messages. I imagined him at home, unable to venture out of his silence. Gradually transforming into a castaway, bearded and remote as he stopped communicating with the outside world. Seeing which cracks he might slip through. I waited until the next Sunday and showed up unannounced bearing a jar of instant coffee, a bag of peaches from the market, and some biscuits. Was he surprised to see me? Impossible to tell.

He looked down at my shoes.

Ah yes.

I pulled them off and threw them onto the heap.

My gifts were welcomed. He hadn't been past the corner shop and would soon be reaching the end of his mother's winter hoard (she was from that generation). In the kitchen, a mosaic of the tilted and dirty, he put on the kettle. We stood in silence listening to the water rouse, and I studied his profile as he poured. His skin looked somewhat weather-beaten, as though from exposure to the elements, and a crescent of faint holes climbed up his ear. When he turned to hand me my tea I noticed the faint trace of a nose ring too.

Down the sombre corridor, into the brightness of the living room.

He was in the midst of a jigsaw puzzle of the solar system, he said, pointing proudly. Ten thousand pieces.

With only Mars and Jupiter to go, it colonised most of the dining table.

So, how did you feel about the memorial?

A bunch of old obsessives.

I saw young people there too.

Old and young obsessives.

Did you know many of them?

About half.

He gestured towards the armchairs. It really was an odd fabric, as though from a nursery, this dark green with purple comets.

The armchairs were angled towards the canal.

Should we . . . ? He pivoted his towards me.

My hand, I can't . . .

He came over to help grip and shift.

And now, face-to-face. The label of my tea bag had fallen inside; he'd poured the water too quickly. I tried to ignore it and rested the mug on my thigh. He set his down on the floor. I blew into my tea and watched the label circle.

My mother would close the curtains when it got dark, he said. She hated the thought of strangers looking in.

But you like having them open?

I have nothing to hide.

And privacy?

What does that even mean?

From where I sat I could see a houseboat lacquered red and black, imperturbable, but no faces at its windows.

So you didn't like the memorial?

Not much.

All those stories and observations. It was very moving.

He shrugged. I wondered whether anyone could indeed see us now, sitting in our armchairs like a long-married couple who'd run out of things to say.

Your mother said you used to work for the NHS.

Yes, at reception.

And how was that?

Great, actually.

Were you there a long time?

Since my late twenties.

And before the NHS?

I was . . . Well . . . Before that I had a few tough years . . .

I was tempted to enquire but thought best to leave it.

And what do *you* do?

Attention averted.

I polish silver.

Cutlery at a fancy home?

No no, in a jewellery shop.

Another pause. It was hard to imagine him answering

the phone at reception; perhaps at work he'd been more forthcoming. I might have felt compelled to fill the silence had it not been for the drone of the television in the background on low volume. It made things comfortable. I sipped my tea, wondered why I had come. But he seemed so alone, and though he didn't show it was perhaps happy for the company. At some point we moved to the sofa. Max brought out a few beers and a bowl of Twiglets. And each time conversation stuttered I stood up and casually walked the room, alert to every trace and detail. The whale mug from the Wellcome plunked down on a Latin dictionary. The strands of coppery hair in a brush on the cabinet. The worn Birkenstocks, the fuchsia scarf draped over a chair, the half-filled ashtray by the phone. Nothing had been cleared away. Was he waiting a bit longer?

On the coffee table sat a pile of books, most of them with bookmarks at different places. Rilke. Novalis. *Emblemata: Handbuch zur Sinnbildkunst des XVI und XVII Jahrhunderts. Spuren*, by Ernst Bloch. A Volvo manual. *An Illustrated History of the Perspective Box. Kinomagie. Servants of the Invisible. Realms of Light.* The collected stories of Rudyard Kipling.

And, next to the books, a pile of pamphlets. I picked up the top one, flicked through its pages. They were newsletters from the Magic Lantern Society.

Take as many as you want, he said.

I stuffed six or seven into my bag.

Take more.

I thought about taking the rest, there were still quite a few, but didn't want to appear greedy. I opened my bag, added four.

He'd soon be embarking on a triage, he said, though

nothing compared to when his mother sold off her collection. That was a historical moment. Afterwards, you could actually cut a straight path through a room and see out of every window and go to sleep without worrying something would fall on your head in the night. I asked why she'd done it. Atonement, he said. By that I supposed he meant the guilt of Jan's death. And after a life of accumulation, he went on, she suddenly developed an obsession with scaling down. Although you would never know if you looked around now, would you? Anyway, he was infinitely relieved, if relief could indeed extend into infinity, when she decided to part with it. That was a remarkable moment, it really was, and he couldn't believe when it actually happened.

Seeing a jump in register, I asked him to tell me, if he liked, about the day his mother parted with her toys.

Well . . . (he fetched another beer, relaxed into the sofa), first a major buyer came along, an industrialist from Frankfurt with a bedridden wife and four young children. Three men arrived on his behalf to empty the warehouse of its contents – peep shows, mirrors and magic lanterns, hundreds of boxes of slides. Was it cathartic? he'd asked. No, it was like having a few essential organs carved out in slow motion, she said as they watched the lorries depart. Next came the library. The shelves at home went from bursting to bare. A momentary pang of regret: so many books, hefty luminous books full of marvellous illustrations, he had never peered into. And now never would. The men came for more boxes. The auction at Criterion lasted three days. Wilhelmina couldn't bear to sit through it but asked for reports of who bought what for how much.

And then came the huge sale, in their home, of all of the

remaining objects, still plenty in number but only a faint echo of the collection. As he helped affix sales tags on the lanterns and shadow puppets, he began to feel a mounting exhilaration. Such exhilaration, he didn't sleep for days. It was like parting from an unwanted sibling. And yet he would never forget the unchecked rapacity that one March Sunday. His mother had sent out word via the Magic Lantern Society newsletter, the ad then reproduced in *The Optical Times* and two smaller magic lantern periodicals in France and Belgium, as well as four antiquarian journals that specialised in optical rarities. Aware of the treasures she had amassed over the decades, aware such occasions were increasingly few, everyone in the community began smacking their lips. You could almost hear them from afar. That morning Max and Wilhelmina laid out twenty-two mugs and a tray of recently expired marzipan. Neither sufficed for all those who streamed in that day, around sixty in all. Every visitor would ring the bell repeatedly and with an impatience no one tried to mask they'd tramp hungrily down the stairs, pausing briefly to take in the view, before starting to paw through a lifetime's obsession. Max watched from his place by the table – he was in charge of refilling the teapot – and his mother watched from a corner, itching to intervene.

Take it all, he kept thinking, take it all, and they seemed to heed his wishes.

The cabinetmaker came with his daughter Orla, whom Max had kissed when he was twelve. They were the only ones who kept their hands to themselves. A man began to rearrange a row of magic lanterns, murmuring something to his companion as new positions were decided on the shelf. A woman in a red felt hat set down her mug of tea on a volume of Cheselden's *Osteographia*. Someone else flipped through a limited edition of Athanasius Kircher, turning the pages rather brusquely. Bold fingers picked at the slots of a zoetrope, gave it a spin. Others sifted through the hanging shadow puppets as though they were clothes on a bargain rack. With preternatural calm, his mother observed them. With a joy he could hardly contain, he did too. The marzipan dwindled on the tray. One by one, and in groups, the objects were spoken for, some removed that day and others set aside to be fetched later with car. Towards the very end of the afternoon, once nearly all of the shelves lay barren, a man with thinning spiky hair and loop earrings appeared and shoved past everyone, muttering loudly. There had been traffic on the motorway, he said, and explained to no one in particular, which meant an elderly man who happened to be standing nearby stirring sugar into his tea, that he was a member of Dead Chickens, a punk collective in Berlin that built monsters out of scrap metal, and it'd occurred to them upon seeing the notice that some of these optical instruments might supply eyes for their machines, it'd be brilliant to add an older gaze to their modern creations, it really would, and might he buy a few of the less expensive instruments to that end? A ripple of horror spread through the room – by now everyone was listening, not only the elderly man – and for the first time that afternoon Wilhelmina spoke. She could no longer contain herself. *Überhaupt nicht.* The old punk shrugged as he reached for the remaining piece of marzipan and shortly afterwards the other visitors, more than satiated, zipped up their jackets and headed out, pushing the Dead Chicken and his wild idea onto the street. And so it was that the collection was dismantled, their family monster laid to rest.

No more tricks, no more abracadabra, no more misdirection or uncertainty, no more seeing things one way while most people saw them another. No more standing in darkened rooms trying to detect the source of something that enters abruptly, demanding attention. No more. And yet there is no such thing as an entirely vacant space. Sensory deprivation experiments have shown that a space completely emptied of signs and objects of perception is swiftly invaded, just think of St Anthony assailed in the desert. He was so happy to be rid of all those hideous things.

His manner had lightened considerably as he'd gone along, lighter and lighter with every stage of dismantling, and he seemed almost ecstatic by the time he finished. Now that he'd opened up a bit I thought of steering the conversation into more personal territory. So how do you spend the days now? He shrugged, then rubbed his eyes the way people do from exhaustion. It was complicated, he said. His mother had left him with all sorts of things to deal with, which were annoying even with the help of family friends and accountant, and he also had to look after house and mouse. Both needed daily upkeep.

I heard the sound of spinning in the background. Perhaps the whole time we'd been talking. Is that the mouse? Ah yes. He sliced a carrot and scooped out a cup of grains and after the mouse had helped himself to both Max held his arm in the tank at a diagonal and let him crawl onto it. He brought the creature over to the sofa, where it quickly disappeared into a crevasse between two cushions. I was scared that any movement of mine might crush him and sat very still, but after a few minutes the mouse resurfaced.

It paused on the armrest, travelled the length of the back, then looped back towards Max. Somehow it knew not to stray too far.

He soon had to pay a visit to Isidore's native country, actually. Was he not a London mouse? Yes, but he came from the Warburg, the place where his mother had worked. Had the mouse been on the payroll too? No, Max replied seriously, and told me how he'd been glimpsed in Periodicals, hurtling past a row of filing cabinets, then a few days later on another floor, and was finally caught beside a facsimile that seemed to have drawn his attention. How did they know it was the same mouse? No one could be sure, but once he was caught, the large book in question ceased to exhibit new paw and tooth marks. Wilhelmina had overheard the handyman and another librarian discussing what to do with him, whether to gently dispose of him or find a way of releasing him into Gordon Square, and as she listened to their deliberations it occurred to her that the mouse was too precious to abandon, he was already part of the archive, so she intervened and brought him home in a carton marked HERO.

And now one of the librarians had rung to say his mother had left a bag. He had to go collect it. Encouraged by how the initial awkwardness had lifted, I said I'd accompany him. He seemed surprised, but smiled and welcomed the offer.

Here, he said, gently transferring the mouse into my hands. The little creature had the weight of a light bulb and felt just as fragile.

Each Magic Lantern Society newsletter came with an insert, four pages printed on matte rather than the glossy paper of the rest, titled 'Sales and Wants'. I soon noted there were many more listings under Sales than Wants, as though people were shy to publicise what they wanted but had no issue announcing what they sought to relinquish. What was for sale? The broken, the redundant, the rejected. And what was sought? The unusual, *I need this too since it tells a story*, and a similar will towards completion of a series I'd seen at the shop.

Wanted
Photographic slides of the North East of England.
Readings for 'The landlord's visit', 'Lottie Lee', 'Jim the crossing sweeper'.
Also song slides, illustrated recitations and hymns. Any slides of coastal fairs.

For Sale
Slides:
Man lying on floor in doorway, waiter with tray trips over him, very good quality.
Lady in chair, monkey behind her, monkey pulls off nightcap, she's bald!

Man reading a newspaper with candle, sets light to his hat.
Man diving off a cliff, dog tries to stop him, tears his coat, dives into oblivion.
Violin player outside house – door opened by butler (very slight paint damage).
Acrobat arches himself for take-off, he succeeds only to tip over and land on his face. Excellent condition.
12-slide set of Beauty and the Beast. Signs of age, not wear.
Complete repair, renovation and general revival service for all wooden lanterns.

'Sales and Wants': a surge in desire followed by a melancholic dip, a constant yen for addition and subtraction, though most of what we want to sell off or acquire is not so tangible or easy to define.

At dusk and dawn my hand still felt stiff, as though lulled into calm or activity and then wrenched from that state and resentful. The scars on my palm were scarcely visible apart from a salamander-shaped mark that had formed at the base of my thumb. I'd continued with the exercises the surgeon had prescribed, movements to improve lymphatic drainage and vascularisation, yet it was taking a while for flexibility to return. At work I stuck to the simplest forms of polishing, relied more than ever on my machine, and hoped none of my colleagues would notice.

For our birthdays each one of us, from till assistant and polisher to head jeweller, would be offered a sixty per cent discount on any item. Every ring of mine therefore represented a year in the shop, messy slabs of life compressed into 925 sterling, so many highs and lows and plateaus of emotion as my zodiac steadily grew: classic skull, cat, bull, bat, kudu, eagle, and a snail whose head would often catch on things as though asking the world to slow down.

It was Kate who cast the rings, copying wax models made years ago, the classic skull and cat two of our oldest. The mould itself, a cube usually, was made of gesso or silicon, and she would pour the wax in one confident go and then tighten the screws and let it set. At fashion school her favourite activity had been cutting patterns; she liked the outline of things, she once said, hollows waiting to be filled, without ever elaborating further. Kate was often hungover – her sister worked at a nightclub in Soho – yet even at her rawest she remained meticulous in her movements, the chaos in her head stilled between her hands. Whenever she was offended, whenever she felt cranky and weary as though the world were against her, she would remind us that her great-grandfather had been one of the last witches to inhabit the woods of Essex. Legend had it he could stop farm machines with a glance, stare at a tractor and bring it to a halt. Long ago she and Paul had a dalliance but they now ignored each other politely, no easy feat in such close quarters but they managed, gallantly limiting their interactions to discussing an item of jewellery or a mould that needed updating, while the rest of us would listen in on their exchanges, hoping for a spot of friction to liven up the afternoon. Over the years I'd warmed to Kate and her prickliness. Ever since my return from Mexico, however, things between us had been strained. I couldn't tell how much stemmed from unhappiness, though her unhappiness rose more from circumstance, I guessed, rather than perpetual affliction; someone once said the tormented person suffers from torment, the narcissistic person from tribulations.

Once our bull ring went missing. From one day to the next, the mould went astray. No one could figure out where it had gone. Stolen by a rival, binned accidentally, or misplaced? Little by little the remaining bulls in our shop were sold off until the very last one was removed from the showcase. Its disappearance led to ever more elaborate speculation. Paul spoke of a nascent minotaur cult. Kate suspected a foreign mission, like those jewellery thieves from Montenegro who would dress in drag and speed off on motorboats.

If I had to choose, the bull ring would be my favourite out of all the animals. Its heft, its curve, the placid gaze and quiet purpose, the way in which its horns brushed the neighbouring fingers when worn. There were actually two bull rings, one had a ring through its nose, which seemed cruel even in silver, and I much preferred the one without. During the months we stopped selling the bull it seemed more special, more mythic, than ever. There was absolute elation the day the mould turned up, mysteriously returned to its box.

When the Blake postcard went missing, I knew it had been Kate. I'd seen her staring at it during moments I was away from my bay. And one day when we were the last two at closing time I finally asked. With the tiniest bit of prompting she opened up to me, as though impatient to confess. Each time she walked past she swore she could hear a nineteenth-century voice calling out *I want! I want!* And she just knew he was addressing her, she was the moon he'd set his sights on, and she couldn't let that cry go unheard. I shook my head, extended a few words of sympathy. I couldn't bring myself to tell her that I too had heard his cry in the past, and resisted a similar impulse.

A nineteenth-century voice: I tried to imagine its timbre. The icy stranger might've paced my thoughts with a heavier tread (though the fur trim would have precluded him from becoming *too* much of an object of fantasy) had I not met Max shortly afterwards and been distracted. Neither had much in common with my most recent infatuation, a stagehand in his late fifties, who every now and then drifted back to mind. In his late fifties, but trapped in adolescent yearnings and a brown leather jacket. I fell under his spell for three months. He'd come into the shop to have his rings polished, a set of three gangster rings. At first I only focused on the silver. My aim wasn't to remove all the murk from the gangsters' faces, it was important to preserve their shadowy nature, just enough to return the radiance to their eyes, that flicker of intention, and as I polished them I was reminded of those American presidents whose faces are chiselled into the mountain rock. I loved portrait rings for this very reason; not only were you restoring the shine but you were heightening an expression, giving it more range and complexity. The gangster rings were the creation of a fancy Chelsea jeweller, not ours, but because the stagehand, who I now noticed was himself of craggy demeanour, was a faithful customer, we would occasionally polish his trove at no additional cost. When I was done I laid the rings out on a velvet board. He seemed pleased with the lustre I'd added to his little accomplices, *my little accomplices*, he called them, and slipped all three onto the fingers of his right hand while depositing the other rings in a black tote bag. And then, still gazing down at his hands, he asked whether I'd be free for a drink after work. Our three-month dalliance, which came to an end one Sunday when we ran into his children's nanny at a flea market, wasn't long or deep enough to warrant any keepsake but before parting he gave me a vintage policeman's cape he'd come across while clearing out his council flat. The cape was a thick black wool and had two lion-head clasps connected by a chain. It will suit you, he said, and left me at the bus stop with the heavy garment weighing down my shoulders. On my way home I noticed it was full of little white cocoons and debated leaving it on the bus, the seat next to me was free, but decided it might come in handy in winter. I hung the cape in the broom closet at the far end of my bedroom, where to this day the moth couture carried on its work.

He had only visited the Warburg once with her, but Wilhelmina would often say that the building was her spiritual home, it transported her to the libraries of Vienna and Berlin, places of her youth, and she dearly hoped it would resist all calls of modernisation. As soon as he'd entered it all felt dizzyingly familiar, the wood panelling, blue-carpeted floors, avuncular filing cabinets, infinity of books. She'd stopped to show him a volume on comets in medieval China and, elsewhere, six rows devoted to Egyptian amulets. Look at these scarabs, she'd said, and these, before leading him to the fourth floor. The fourth was her favourite, where the meteorology books complicated the air.

Outside his hermitage, I noticed, Max was more balanced in conversation, though he still had a tendency to leap from silence into overdrive, like the mouse on its wheel, as if he knew no mode in between, and as we walked down Cartwright Gardens, which turned into Marchmont Street, home to Judd Books and a string of languishing cafes, and then onto Tavistock Place moving towards Woburn Square, he told me about the puzzle he was working on, a six-thousand-piece desert landscape, very challenging as I could imagine what with the lack of variation, and then segued into a discussion of films that were set in the desert, from *Lawrence of Arabia* to *Mad Max* to *Walkabout*.

As we drew near our destination we saw a brick edifice covered in scaffolding. There it was, obscured by a dense grid of metal poles intersected by wooden planks. Attached to the structure, a sign: WARBURG RENAISSANCE. HONOURING OUR PAST, BUILDING OUR FUTURE. Up the ramp and into the foyer, to be greeted by a tall fern, a replica of a Grecian frieze of the muses, journals in vitrines, and the word MNEMOSYNE carved above the entrance. Our momentum, for we were walking quite nicely apace, was brought to a halt by the woman at reception who sat behind a clear plastic screen that seemed to refute any pull of antiquity. My mother used to work here, said Max. Wilhelmina Blau. No reaction. Wilhelmina Blau, he said again. I wondered whether she'd heard him but moments later, summoned by a means unknown, another woman appeared, with a thick braid and forest-green skirt. She introduced herself as Miranda, one of the librarians, and had been at the memorial and looked for Max afterwards. She handed him his mother's bag.

Might he, now that he was here, have a look around? The building was in the midst of a grand renovation, she said, but if we didn't mind a bit of dust . . . We followed her past walls of hanging sheets as she spoke about Aby Warburg, addressing me since Max may have been familiar with his story, a singular, and really quite brilliant, art historian from Hamburg whose collections of books and images were the foundation of this institute. She paused in front of a portrait – the name Aby somehow matched the dark-eyed melancholy of the man – flanked by his loyal companions, there's Fritz Saxl, there was Gertrud Bing, friends and archivists who helped organise the transfer of his library from Germany to England and not a moment too soon, Warburg didn't live long enough to witness the horrors, but . . . A loud drilling started up on the floor above. Well, let's move on, she said, and led us into a tiny lift. The third floor had already undergone its transformation, floors of new red linoleum and bright strip lights overhead. The woman pointed to a three-tiered shelf on wheels labelled 'Books for Shelving' and said Wilhelmina had loved shelving books, in fact it had been her favourite activity since it gave her an excuse to spend more time in the stacks and she was forever curious to see what people were reading.

I tried to imagine Isidore's routes; so many corners and corridors, so much nesting material, everywhere you turned.

The library was divided across four floors – IMAGE WORD ORIENTATION ACTION – four categories into which, I couldn't help thinking, daily life might be organised too. Max asked for the bathroom and left me to wait by the shelves. My eyes fell on a book. *Medieval Man and his Notions*. Intrigued to see how different medieval man might have been from the modern, what notions he followed and whether he was any wiser than my contemporaries, I opened to a random page. There was a list of the personalities a baby boy would inherit depending on when he was born during the lunar cycle. If born on day 4, he would be false in words. On day 5, 17 or 20, he would have an early death. A long life was guaranteed if born on day 6 or 7, while day 18 or 19 ensured happiness. If born on day 23, he would turn to thieving and roguery. Yet these prophecies were nuanced by others, since character was believed to also be determined by the day of the week on which the child was born. Sunday: handsome, no anxiety.

Wednesday: sharp, bitter and cautious in word. Friday . . . Miranda the librarian began to explain the ways in which they had improved the space, look at these strip lights, and these brand-new lamps with brand-new bulbs, and look at the nice hinge we've created between Mathematics and Divination . . . I returned the book to the shelf.

Back on the ground floor she gave us a quick tour of the Reading Room, where she showed us a facsimile of the vast atlas Warburg created after spending several years in psychiatric institutions. Nearly one thousand images spread over sixty-three black panels, in which he juxtaposed reproductions of artworks with newspaper cuttings, celestial maps, coins, calendars and commercials, everything part of his own retelling of civilisation, human drama and its visual undertow, and in this ordered delirium he demonstrated how gestures were often repeated, say a certain pose on an ancient coin resurfacing, centuries later, on a postage stamp. Aby Warburg remained elusive even to scholars who'd dedicated their lives to him. This atlas was the closest they'd ever get to a map of his mind. I thought I saw a stirring in Max's eyes as he gazed at the pages. And an idea began to form.

Old paper loses moisture over time, the corners start to curl, but it still provides insulation. Easier to shred are the contents of middle-aged books, especially ones printed in Italy, which continue to collect moisture and are kinder on the teeth. But really, any kind of paper, young or old, provides decent furnishing for a nest.

There was much more interesting nesting material in his old home. Life was, he must admit, close to perfect. Every now and then from the deceptive immensity of his new glass enclosure — there seems to be little between him and the rest of the room and yet he slides down each time he tries to climb the walls — he transports himself there:

Most mornings, shortly after his nocturnal activities had come to a close, he'd be roused by the roar of a long-nosed machine being pushed across the carpet, alerting him to the arrival of the other species. He'd scurry into one of the many entrances to the netherworld, this one carved out by an unknown predecessor to whom he was forever indebted, and settle into a longer nap until evening. Only once all footsteps had faded and the mouse's kingdom had returned to silence would he creep out to explore any changes brought by the day. He was thankful for the carpet's ocean of blue, the spring of the stools, and the underbellies of the footed filing cabinets that created wonderful roofs, only he wished he could swing from the hanging light switches, which dangled just out of reach. His favourite floor was PERIODICALS, fitted with cool, dark spaces, also prized for its proximity to the tea room.

Life continued along its daily circuits until one day another universe appeared. Laid out on a table in the Reading Room. A sky of black with constellations scattered across it. The surface was sweeping and shiny and smelled, unlike the other books in the library, of fresh ink. A new arrival from a foreign land. Cautiously he chewed a corner, wasn't certain of the taste, but found himself returning. More than the taste of the book, however, it was the images it held. It may not have had the depth of tunnels or corridors but its scale was appealing: he was astonished to discover that individuals of the other species were now smaller than himself. He was bigger than the figures under his paws. Some of these figures seemed to be in unnatural positions, others looked very angry or sad. Every now and then his hind paws would step on the feet of a female with long, flowing hair, nearly as beautiful as the delicate white mouse he once glimpsed on floor three, and they would form a duo, the mouse and the image beneath.

The mouse wasn't the only one who seemed to have fallen under the spell of the crepuscular book. Each night he'd find it open to a different part and could see fingerprints all over it, smell the presence of other beings. His visits must have been noticed too. One evening as he rushed along, impatient to burrow into its pages, he jumped onto the table and soon met a dead end. His movements were arrested by some kind of wall. Another wall closed over his head. Sudden darkness. The next morning someone lifted the top, quickly shut it again. Commotion around the box. Movement. No movement. He curled into a tight ball and feared the worst, feared someone might think of using his tail like one of those cloth strings that hung out of old books . . . and what would they do with the rest of him?

But disaster was not to follow. Only change. Which, depending on how you saw it, was a quieter form of disaster.

A new home, and large calloused hands that would cup him into their warm, tobacco darkness.

In his new home, there are no long corridors, no corners to veer round, no paper to shred, only pine shavings. No more surprises, no variation, apart from that the large, warm hands have been replaced by colder, smaller ones that lift him out and stroke him daily with an enthusiasm that borders on obsession. What does he know about obsession? There were gestures in the great book. He is fed, his water bottle replenished, his home cleaned often enough. Occasionally he is let out, although not as frequently as he would like. The muscles in his paws and his incisors twitch. His eyes follow the movements of the other species.

In a corner of our workshop, at the far end where the ceiling dropped and you had to crouch down to avoid bumping your head, lived the burly electric kettle and its coterie of mugs. A few steps from this area resided the pickle jar, our name for the vat of ultrasonic solution in which every ring, chain and pendant would be soaked once done with the process of soldering. After visiting the jar, your hands now emptied, you'd prepare yourself a cup of tea. I never got used to the act of dropping in the pieces and letting them sink to the bottom, the sense that now that I'd finished my job it was being taken over by a colleague who worked in obscurity. I could imagine the *pez diablo* at home in its murky depths, these depths into which we tossed the fruits of our labour. What in heavens is that? Paul had asked when he saw it pinned to the wall. I've brought us a mascot, I said, admiring how in our semi-lit realm the thing looked even more devilish, its dark mood undiluted. Caught, carved and laid out to dry into something demonic. Its mother would have once terrorised a Mexican lake, unaware that one of her children would end up as a curio.

Every drop contains its mother. The phrase returned on my lunch break as I sat on the step with my tea and sandwich, happy no one had come out to join me. A well-dressed man walked past, the belt from his jacket trailing the ground. Excuse me . . . but the man didn't hear me and walked on. A few moments later, a mother and daughter limped past in tandem, and I couldn't help wondering whether they had perhaps suffered an accident on a bicycle for two that had tipped over and crushed each left leg at the exact same spot, or else they were so intimately entwined, the way twins often are, that one's affliction had been transferred to the other. I thought of my own mother, and how at first we'd limped in tandem after my father disappeared, the one moment in life when our gait was matched, our movements slowed through space and time, but we hadn't maintained the same rhythm for long. I suspected Max and Wilhelmina had also moved through life at a different pace. Wilhelmina. I found myself missing that startling focus, almost tautness, she'd brought to existence. Once she was gone, life slipped back into a much more familiar laxity. As for Max, he occupied the far end of the spectrum. Tug and repose. Then again, another's grief is impossible to measure. I remembered that from when an uncle passed away. Some of my cousins had gone mad with grief and confronted it head-on while others went along as though nothing had changed, wearing their sadness like those external pockets people used to have in other centuries, tied to a string and never fully integrated into the clothing; only years later, when it had all grown too heavy, would they burst.

She often rang at irksome times.

Did I wake you? she always asked.

No.

I forget the time difference, sorry.

I let her continue.

How is your hand?

Mending pretty well, I think.

You've gone back to work?

Yes, since I returned.

Does it still hurt?

I have twinges. How is Diogenes?

Still mopey but eating a little better.

I hadn't realised he wasn't eating enough.

Yes, since his surgery. You know, we snipped him.

Yes, I remember.

And how is everything else, anything nice to report?

I think my landlords might not raise the rent.

That's good news . . . But you *are* looking after your hand?

It's mending well, I repeated.

And you're doing your exercises?

Every morning. And then, before she could further enquire, I've met someone interesting.

I could hear her listening more intently.

Is that so?

Well, I'm not sure it's anything worth reporting.

Whoever it is, dear, give him a chance. Oh, actually, Flora, I'd better go now. Look after your hand, darling, and yourself.

My stepfather had entered the room.

There'd been no signs of anything brewing or gathering but the storm must have been heading over while I cooked supper, bathed, chatted to a friend. I had just slipped into bed with a book when there was a loud thunderclap and from one moment to the next the windows were lashed by rain. The lights flickered and went out, leaving the room in darkness. When the lights flickered back on I noticed a chunky spider on the wall, as though delivered by the clap of thunder. Perhaps it had come inside in search of somewhere dry. I had no problem with smaller spiders, but past a certain size they felt like an intrusion. And it was one thing to watch a spider mature, if it started out in its corner as a spiderling and then slowly turned into something formidable you at least had time to grow used to it and even form an attachment, but another matter to find an adult spider, brazenly there. This one was black and shiny like a clump of wet tea leaves. It moved across the wall at alarming speed, leaving an invisible spider trail behind it, writing its presence all over the wall. Without another thought I ran downstairs, immensely relieved to find my landlord in the living room. He was a guarded, solemn man. A barrister, before retirement.

There's a spider, a rather large one . . . There was no need to finish my sentence. He put aside his book and followed me up to my rooms. The spider was now on my pillow, a twitchy calligraphy against the white. The lights flickered again. We heard a crackle and then the pop of a power fuse as a lamp went out in the corner. Oh dear, we may have to call an electrician, my landlord said as he shook the spider to the floor and captured it with a glass and paper. He went over to the window and with some difficulty tossed it into the night as wind and rain fought to enter.

He laid down the glass on the table. Another thunderclap. I hoped it wasn't delivering more spiders. We moved away from the window just as all the lights went out now, leaving us in near total darkness until a flash of lightning violently illuminated the room and where my landlord stood I saw for an instant another man, shorter in height, stockier in frame, hair tapered at the sides. The face, long dead to me, was staring in my direction, and during that moment of illumination so many emotions swept over me, rage and adoration and an awful kind of terror. They continued to thrive in the darkness that followed the flash, and I could see him turning away towards the window, as though even now, even now, he was reluctant to approach. And then one more clap of thunder, less mighty than the last, and the lights returned, obliterating the figure. That was something, wasn't it? said my landlord with a nervous laugh as he walked to the door.

Under a constellation of hanging cone lights, Max waved me over to his corner of the pizzeria. He'd combed his hair into some kind of quiff and wore two loop earrings, his eighties look amplified by a black polo shirt and jean jacket. Hi, Flora, hi, he said a little hopelessly. It wasn't only his appearance that sparked unease. As soon as I took my seat I noticed there were crumbs on the tablecloth, a crumpled napkin at my place, the damp imprint of a mouth on the rim of my glass of water. I'd walked through the door only moments ago yet began to suspect that a few minutes earlier someone else had been sitting where I now sat. I asked Max whether someone had been there. No, it was just him and Ray, and he held up an old paperback of *The Martian Chronicles*. The waiter brought bread, olive oil and a little dish. He poured some of the oil into the dish, making a point, for my benefit I couldn't help feeling, that he was doing this all at our table for the first time that evening. Max studied the wine list and after much pondering ordered a bottle of house red. He tore off a hunk of bread, dipped it in oil. Ate more bread, went quiet. There was something peaceful about him, in his anxious reticence; he lacked his mother's rigour, but her continuous company may have been exhausting.
¡Hola, Flora!

My friend Pato, who had the gift of ubiquity and would cycle round London and pop up in the most unexpected of places, had entered the pizzeria. Upon seeing me he came over. Pato, Max. Max, Pato. They sized one another up – Max seated, Pato standing – and Max nodded curtly. Pato, speaking from his cloud of exuberance, began telling me about his latest project, a triptych that would involve a Greek sculpture, a Chilean poet and a seventies rock song. If I were to shake my London deck and see which rogue card came tumbling out, it would have Pato's image etched on the front. He represented something else, a foreign land I could travel back to while also keeping my Spanish alive. He too had grown up fatherless, his lost to a motorcycle crash on the outskirts of Santiago. One of his most recent paintings, which had caught my eye, was called *Self-Portrait as Studio at Night*. A long hand extends out of the window of a tree house resting on a leafy crest. Inside you see classical ruins and fragments of sculptures and jars of paintbrushes. It's hard to tell where the roof ends and the pitchy sky begins, there seems to be a flow between everything, and then you look down to see a deep cleft running through the street below, as though it were about to split in two, and there stand three very tall street lamps whose silvery emissions illuminate everything around them, but the streets are desolate, there's no one to be seen at this hour of the night, no one to intrude upon the tower and the sanctuary and the ruins that are the walls and ceiling and splintered floor of the artist's mind.

Pato carried on . . . Aphrodite, Huidobro, a song by Television . . . Every now and then I'd nod to indicate I was listening. It'd happened to me in the past, many times, that when someone went on and on I would start to get an idea, just when I was expected to pay attention to someone else's thoughts I would indulge my own and enter them more deeply, the focus moving inwards when required to shift out, and often that bit of resistance proved fertile ground. In fact, many of my best ideas, apart from when I sat polishing, had been born from moments I'd been a captive audience. And so it was that as Pato outlined the particulars of his new triptych, which really did sound exciting, I fine-tuned the idea that'd started to form at the Warburg, shuffling through images from the past few months, each an unfinished story shedding its own tenuous light, each slightly teasing, a slight stretch of reality, all part of a bid, perhaps, for a new perspective.

Anyway, I'll catch you soon, Pato said after a few minutes and, unaware of how his intervention had assisted my thinking, walked off to join his friend. Max and I ordered a mushroom pizza and, eventually, another bottle of wine. Towards the end of the evening, anxious to return to my idea, I asked how his mother had acquired this lantern of hers, the one I'd brought back from Mexico. As expected, he promptly set out on one of his memory tracks, and while he waxed lyrical about his childhood, piling on the detail, I continued to mentally tinker, impressed by how skilled I'd become at listening to someone else and to myself at the same time.

Dutch women at their windows, rags in hand. Always at their windows. Whenever he thought about Holland, his memories began there, with these women they'd see on their morning walks. Every late June they'd drive over from Germany in Wilhelmina's station wagon to stay with Jan's family. They'd stop for nourishment and strolls in Arnhem,

Utrecht and Gouda, and arrive in The Hague past bedtime. Whatever the hour, whatever the mood, Jan's family would be waiting up for them with food and drink. On the kitchen wall, alongside the cast-iron *poffertjes* pan, hung a wooden spoon used for discipline. His cousin Karel, with whom he shared a bunk bed, lived in piggy anticipation of one, and in fear of the other. After breakfast Max and his parents would drive along the Strandweg and park the car by the Kurhaus from where they'd walk to the perpetually windy beach of Scheveningen, the only important beach of his life, its carousel and windy currents superimposed onto every beach that came afterwards. There were also sand dunes, beautiful ridges shaped over time by the wind. In the first half of the twentieth century this place had been home to the fanciest seaside resort in Holland, in fact the Nazis, in their perverse love of installing evil within elegance, would haunt this beach and could easily be identified by the way they pronounced *Scheveningen*, an immediate giveaway. His mother had never mastered the word either. After the war the place was abandoned by grandeur and fell into something like ruin, and in its new incarnation it became a magnet for northern Germans and pallid pensioners who were wheeled around by their nurses. But the sun rarely lasted and often all they got was a diet of rain and wind with a few timid sunbeams since just as everyone had relaxed onto their towels a dark cloud would appear followed by a downpour, hardly an interlude between, and people would have to pack up and hurry back to their accommodations. The sea always looked grey, rarely blue, and he never felt like entering the chilly, choppy water.

We could put on the show in the workshop, yes, that would be the perfect place, wouldn't it, even if we couldn't ensure total darkness it would probably be dark enough if we turned off all the lights and closed the door at the top of the stairs.

People would bring their own *broodjes* and novels by Couperus. (His father would say that you couldn't claim to be Dutch if you hadn't read Couperus, Couperus ran through the veins of his people like canal water.) Others would visit the stands selling herrings and frites although these too, like the restaurants on the promenade, had to hurry and close whenever the wind got out of hand. Along with sun chairs you could rent shields against the wind, that's how strong the gales were, and even when shut the metal signs outside businesses continued to rattle, buffeted like the gulls by the currents, and he once watched a book somersault all the way across the beach. In the autumn, emptied of the summer multitudes, Scheveningen would recover some of its elegance, the old man at the hotel reception always tried to reassure them with the help of some crumpled photographs.

We'd also have to think about which slides to project. Certainly some of the ones Wilhelmina had shown in Mexico. Maybe all of them. How many of them could I remember? A nun, a monk, a dancing skeleton, Carlota . . .

Say it, Max said to me. Scheveningen.

He laughed when I tripped over the syllables.

During those stays his parents would never fail to take him to the Mauritshuis, where Wilhelmina would visit her favourite paintings and ignore the rest, art grazing, not gazing, Jan would jest as she singled out the brown wintry landscapes by Avercamp, known in his day as 'the Mute of Kampen', and tell Max to find the lone dogs and graffiti in a church by Saenredam.

But he'd never liked museums. You enter each landscape

but only halfway. You meet each figure, in some cases even lock eyes, but there's no conversation. You are shown a letter but from where you stand you can't read what is written. You are shown a goblet but denied the wine.

It was taking him a while as usual to get to the point, no mention yet of any lantern, but it was just as well since I continued plotting. At the memorial someone had said that Wilhelmina sometimes liked to dress up. I knew just the thing Max could wear. The black policeman's cape. It would surely fit him. He might grow hot in it after a while but it would spill so nicely over his shoulders, lend a bit of grandeur and authority.

There was one more place they would visit: the antiques market on Lange Voorhout. And near that market, one shop in particular, run by an old man named Intlekoffer. He would be seated when they arrived as though he hadn't moved from that spot since their last visit. Overhead, a bunch of Indonesian shadow puppets hung from hooks in the ceiling. They always looked so hungry, the shadow puppets. Better fed were the battalions of tin soldiers in eternal showdowns on the shelves, or sitting on thimble-sized chairs attending the Yalta Conference. Nearby, propped against the wall, would be a row of nineteenth-century African masks; the only one he remembered was of a tax collector from Liberia. Intlekoffer would manage the shop while his wife sat in a corner of the room fixing her dolls. There was always one in her lap when they came in, a shadow rising around each doll like the stamp of a former playmate. Some were so big they looked like children, and she'd sit detangling their hair, picking out the snarls. He once saw her weave a wig straight into the scalp of one, another time she was reattaching the limbs that had severed due to the snap of a string, or fixing the counterweight eyes that rocked open and closed depending on the angle at which the doll was held. Intlekoffer and his wife spent all day together yet slept on opposite sides of the canal, their discontent, if that's what it was, spelled out in the narrow body of water, by turns misty and windswept.

On second thoughts, the cape might be a bit large and full of moths. And he really would get rather hot and be distracted from the show. We wouldn't want that. Operating the lantern will require his full attention. I'd ask him how he felt about the cape rather than make that sort of decision myself, it might not strike his fancy at all, and he did seem to have his own odd fashion sense and might not want me imposing my own.

On the afternoon Wilhelmina bought the Falk magic lantern from Intlekoffer they had driven on to Scheveningen. His mother was captivated by her new toy, kept turning it over in her hands and opening the hatch at the back. There were older children playing on the beach, a volleyball game that seemed to dominate every corner and curve, so he went to walk along the outer fringes of the coastline, towards the hinterland, where it was quieter. No one seemed to notice. It was a nice walk at first, the beach close and distant at once, and he began thinking about a toy soldier, forged from heavy lead, he wished he'd asked his parents to buy. Maybe it would still be there the next time. He was thinking about this soldier when he felt his foot sink in the sand. With the next step, his other foot sank too. The ground beneath him was no longer holding his weight and within seconds he was in past his ankles, then past his knees. He was going down. Into the dune. He was in past his waist now. He tried to reach out and grab on to something but nothing was within reach. He'd once heard of a boy who'd drowned in a sand dune and now it was happening to him. Sand poured into his eyes, and he couldn't even cry out since his mouth too was full of sand. He heard frantic screams, muffled through layers of time. Something, someone, seized his shoulders. More hands. There were now many hands at him, too many to count. It took four men to extract him from the sand. A girl had seen him sink and cried for help. His father and three other men had come running. Someone had appeared with a shovel and thanks to this collective panic he was brought back to the surface. His father cleared the grains from his eyes with a wet cloth. At what point did his mother reappear? He couldn't remember. That night, once his parents had gone to bed, he peered into the lantern sitting on the kitchen table. Inside was nothing more than four tin walls and an oval bulb. Where was the inner life? There must be something his eyes failed to take in.

Yes, it was a splendid idea, despite this unfortunate association, for him to put on a show.

One of the newsletters contained a piece on German toy manufacturers from Nuremberg. Of the many illustrious toymakers from the region, the author devoted several paragraphs to the most modest of them all: Johann Falk. I'd recognised the name and shown Max. This Johann Falk, also known as Joseph and Jean, had created lanterns around the year 1900. His toy-making life began when employed as a travelling agent for the company Carette, of electric toy tram and brass steam engine fame, and after several years of experience he founded his own tin toy business in 1895, at Solgstrasse 19. A firm of twenty-three men and twenty-six women. A few years later a merchant by the name of Moritz Kaumheimer became his partner. *Solidly crafted lanterns with no special features*, was how the author described Falk's creations. They were easy to purchase, available in both toy shops and opticians, and no one thought of them as Jewish lanterns since they were fully assimilated into every collection. Other Jewish toymakers from Nuremberg included the Bing brothers, known for their toy trains, and Spier & Söhne, famous for their board games and picture books. Heinrich Berolzheimer had a well-known pencil factory.

During the First World War, toy production was halted. An official decree insisted that all industrial activities turn to armament production. Magic lantern making was put on hold. Once production resumed, times had changed, new media was on the rise, and there was hardly any demand. And then in the early 1930s, heavier shadows than the ones it had known fell upon the workshop. Falk began to lose clients. Professional relationships would collapse from one day to the next and before long he was pressured into selling his creations for a pittance. In the end, he was one of twenty-nine Nuremberg toymakers, including Bing and Spier, forced to sell off their firms. A certain Ernst Plank took over the company in March 1936; it ceased to exist a year later. Many Jewish inventors were sent away. Some never returned. Yet their toys would have made their way across Europe, ending up in shops, skips or on the shelves of antiquarians. Eight Falks from Nuremberg perished in the Shoah, yet this particular Falk left Germany for England in January 1934 and from there emigrated to New York. He was still waiting for his citizenship papers when he died in 1942 at the age of seventy. It is unknown what sort of work he undertook in the United States, what sort of circle of friends he formed, whether he brought any of his lanterns from Europe, whether he ever put on shows for other émigrés.

There was also one Rabbi Falk — no connection? — who in his London Bridge laboratory had tried to fashion golems out of mud from the Thames.

This last note about Rabbi Falk, gleaned from elsewhere and perhaps pertaining to an entirely different man, was what swayed him. Max would put on a show, and I would help him go through the slides. The idea that'd begun to form at the Warburg, and been given shape at the pizzeria, had continued to knock. At first he'd resisted, as I suspected he would, and said he'd never gone near her things. His mother liked to hint — he never knew how seriously — that the shows were her way of bringing back friends she missed as well as conjuring people she would have liked to have met. He had no interest in doing either. Not even your parents? *Especially* not my parents. I told him about drawings I'd once seen made by people after a loss, individuals who had never drawn anything in their lives seized by the need to create, and mentioned an engraving in his kitchen of a monkey operating a magic lantern. Even a monkey. At the end of our walk — we'd circled Highbury Fields a few times and paused at one of the benches — Max accepted. But added I shouldn't expect anything magnificent. Of course I did not expect much at all. Along with a growing desire to test things a little and give them a push, I'd been struck by how he'd quietly lit up over Warburg's atlas, and decided this might be a way, simply or slightly perversely, to pull him out of his lethargy.

Two silhouettes, stepping out of the frame of another time. A man and a woman. The woman is taller and broader and carries a cane. They are deep in conversation, oblivious to the old trees gathered round. Somehow Max knew it was Aby Warburg and his own mother. Perhaps it was the way she held on to her cane, an object so familiar he could distinguish it from every other cane. Its wood held the imprint of countless walks mother and son had taken together, rarely a moment of silence between the running commentary and the tap tap tap, and whenever they paused to rest at a cafe she would prop the cane beside her at the table so its beak peered over the edge. He remembered the way all of her weight would shift onto it when after a long day out they would board the bus home. And what about Aby, how did he know it was him? Well, he just did, the way one does in dreams, and then there was his agitated step, as though seized by a thought he mustn't let slip out of sight.

That Sunday I agreed to meet him at one of the entrances to the New River Walk – neither new, nor a river, but a man-made channel – and we followed its winding contours in an attempt to retrace the steps of the two figures in his dream, a dream he'd had after our last conversation. The footpath was desolate apart from two ducks collecting furnishings for their home. Yellow leaves and a metallic-red wrapper floated on the cloudy water. In winter many of the trees that lined the bank had lost their foliage, revealing mansions on the other side that were hidden in summer, secretive slumbering homes that seemed to store darkness. Halfway along our walk we came upon the watchman's hut, a round brick edifice with a pointy roof and a shuttered window of an eye. His mother used to tell him all kinds of stories about the New River Walk. It was here that the writer Charles Lamb once lost a friend – blind, the man had walked into the water after paying him a visit at his nearby cottage. And a minister from Newington Green Unitarian Church drowned himself after attacking his wife, a woman of letters, in a spell of madness. Also long ago, young chimney sweeps would come to bathe here on Sundays. To think that from this body of water containing soot and suicides and all other kinds of trauma, much of London used to drink.

I sensed a hidden pact between everything, a density forced open for an instant. Winter branches wrote their foreign messages overhead. A blackbird. A wren. Birds who had stayed behind, not answering to any migratory call. Yet the human species appeared to be obeying some sort of winter brief, and for a long stretch it was only the wind that walked ahead of us. As we neared the end of the path I thought I glimpsed a stooped figure about to turn the bend, a thickset silhouette taking in the winter sun. I was about to say something but the figure vanished from sight. Only later, once we'd left, did I suspect we had arrived late for an appointment.

The cats followed my movements with expectant eyes. One of them meowed. No snacks for you now, I said softly, and no time for petting either. I turned up the music, removed my sweater and brassiere, and wandered about my flat searching for something captivating to wear. Rarely did I dress to captivate, mostly I liked to dress down, but I felt increasingly invested in my pursuits. I tried on one outfit after another. A knee-length skirt. A longer one. A woollen turtleneck dress. After much deliberation, I settled on a pair of black fitted jeans. Nearly there. Just needed to decide on a top. I paused by the window and looked out absent-mindedly, as if able to read the temperature from the mass of clouds and roof silhouettes, and was startled to see a bearded man staring from across the garden. I was aware of how easy it was to look into other people's homes in the early-winter dusk, every lit window like a doll's house, but that evening I'd forgotten to draw the curtains. The man was staring intently. In a panic I grabbed one of the cats, whoever was closer, which meant Pouncer since Lurker was two timid steps behind, and held her up to my bare breasts, her warm pulse against my chest. The closest I would ever come, I knew, to wearing fur.

I could have shown up in a cloth sack and Max would not have noticed. He didn't even ask me to take off my shoes. All his attention was riveted on a high-necked amber bottle on the dining table, right at the centre of Jupiter, the jigsaw now complete. Earlier that day he'd made a discovery, a large cache of whiskey, what forensic officers would call significant, in a wooden chest at the back of his mother's wardrobe. Twelve bottles of Czech single malt standing upright, the way whiskey should be stored. He filled a tumbler for me and topped up his own and solemnly said, Here's to my mother. The whiskey burned and soothed and expanded. Next he produced a pack of cigarettes. The package was red, with the letters ROTH-HÄNDLE in an antiquated font, and an east-pointing hand. His mother had smoked Roth-Händle and only Roth-Händle, a filterless dark tobacco originally so strong people would call it *Lungentorpedo* or *Roter Tod*. She never let him try them. But he had now found two cartons in the chest with the whiskey and could smoke to his lungs' content. I joined him in raising another glass, this time to the visible and invisible and everything in between, and let him light my cigarette, the hospital craving for tobacco yet to be satisfied, feeling its clutch as I inhaled.

The whiskey wasn't the only new presence in the room. To one side of the coffee table stood a tall box with a commanding word. AUTOPERIPATETIKOS. A walking doll his parents had bought for him on a trip to New York – in America, in its hatred of idleness, walking toys were apparently all the rage. He thought it'd stayed behind in Germany but he discovered it in the closet by the whiskey. He lifted the doll out of the box to show me. Her expression was benevolent, with arched eyebrows and a rosebud mouth. Yet this doll, still or in motion, had stolen hours of his sleep when he was a child. Even when his mother hid the key he kept expecting her to whirr back to life. Because of her he'd grown wary of his rocking horse, which advanced twenty-five centimetres with every rock.

On previous visits the lantern had been out on a shelf, but that day it was nowhere to be seen. My eyes kept returning to the spot where it usually lived, between a stack of records and a mantel clock. I scoured the other shelves and tables, every flat surface in the room. It wasn't until I went over to greet the mouse that I saw what Max had done. He'd placed the lantern in the tank, opened the hatch, removed the light source and filled the interior with fresh straw. A miniature ruin with its own chimney and four walls. The mouse was napping inside, in a nest of shredded papers.

Max, we're going to need this lantern for the show, I said. He went over and tipped the sleeping mouse out of the hatch.

Evening hammered at the door. We ignored it. The lantern slides sat in their boxes. We ignored them. Isidore awoke from his nap and spun on his wheel. We began our travels through Wilhelmina's record collection, mostly krautrock from the seventies. Neu! CAN. Faust. Popul Vuh. More whiskey. A few more Roth-Händles. Each drag an assault on the lungs, a tug that made you feel more alive but also seven minutes closer to the grave. At one point someone — a neighbour, most likely — rang the doorbell repeatedly. We ignored it. The music, the whiskey, the violent cigarette: it had been a while since I'd experienced such a swell. *Focus on something red*, a hypnotist who'd once helped me quit smoking had said, on anything from a pair of painted lips to a bottle cap, but in this case the reddest thing in the room was the pack of cigarettes itself.

I marvelled at how Max moved about the space, discreetly keeping his distance. Like an animal in the wild. And for a moment I found myself wishing I could anaesthetise him with a dart from afar, experience what it'd be like to be close to him, then step back as he started to awaken. He lifted the walking doll off her frame. Look, he said, she's little more than a ceramic head mounted on a barrel with a clockwork mechanism and wheels.

In the bathroom I splashed water on my face and then dried it on what turned out to be a pair of trousers hanging from a nail where a towel should have been. I took a step back and nearly tripped over a box of washing powder and wondered, for the sake of my skin, how often the trousers and the washing powder would meet. On my return to the living room, emboldened by the whiskey, I went into a room that'd been closed on every visit. The door opened onto a chilly space unwarmed by any human body in a while, yet when I turned on the light it seemed so busy with little figures I had the sensation I was intruding on a miniature kingdom that'd been going about its daily life. The surfaces teemed with objects, each telling a story I'd never know: a mermaid with crown and guitar, a blue marble obelisk, a plaster owl on a stand, an antique hourglass in an ornate wooden frame, a panel painted with Indian deities, a taxidermied duck's head on a pedestal, a wooden model of a staircase, a row of miniature metal boots with painted heels, a beaded tiger, two wooden matchboxes with scarab designs, a toy paper circus, the papier mâché head of a man in a fez, a tiny porcelain typewriter, a dragon candlestick. At the far end of a shelf, in shadow even with the light on, stood a framed photograph of a man with wavy hair, round wire-rimmed glasses and a careful smile. Formal, rigid, slightly self-conscious: the pose of a daguerreotype. I saw some of Max in him, or rather some of him in Max. My head began to spin as I leaned in to have a closer look. Steady yourself, Flora, steady yourself without further delay. I scanned the room for something neutral. Too much stimulation, everywhere. A dark blue suitcase sat in the corner. It must have been the suitcase she took to Mexico. I walked towards it. The objects on the shelves started to teeter and stir, each step of mine causing very slight tremors. There was no option but to be properly horizontal. The bed was right there. In fact, a corner of it was nudging my knee. I collapsed onto it. Which felt more like into it. But I only sank a few inches. And then stopped. I was lying on a waterbed. Wilhelmina slept on a waterbed, its elusive contours concealed under a knitted blanket. How perverse to seek that loss of solidity when your son sank in sand and your husband drowned in water. My jeans felt tight. I unzipped them. The heating in the house was minimal. Was I even cold? So many closed spaces around me, spaces calling out to be opened, and objects calling out to be contemplated, endless contents awaiting attention. Here I was. In her space. And not only in her space but in her bed. In her bed, my head on her pillow, her very pillow with the coppery imprint of her hair, I now saw, on the pillowcase. It was strange to think she had gazed upon my face more recently than anything in her own room. I closed my eyes and was back in the hospital, with nurses circling and the pump of gel fastened to the door. Wilhelmina was out in the corridor waiting for me to arrive, waiting to resume our conversation. Somewhere in the room was a bread roll hardening in a crumpled napkin.

I heard sounds at the door. I opened my eyes and there was Max. I zipped up my jeans seconds before he grabbed my arm and pulled me off the bed. Careful with my hand, I said. Careful, I repeated, as he hauled me out of the room, no time to bid farewell to anything, and he didn't loosen his grip until the living room, where I collapsed into the sofa and finished off my whiskey. He went to stand by the window. After a few minutes I hoisted myself up, still a bit widdershins, and went over. The lamps along the canal threw ripples of light onto the water and the houseboat windows glowed honeycomb. What were you doing in my mother's room? he asked without turning. I needed to lie down for a moment. There's plenty of space here. Too far. What do you mean too far? My head was spinning, I had to lie down. You know, you have to get over this obsession with her. Don't think I don't know what drives you here, again and again. How do you know it's the only thing? Before he could reply, if that was his intention, I laid my good hand on his cheek and seeing that he didn't move away I brought his face to mine and I kissed him, I sensed a wilderness and felt an urge to fill it or at least alleviate it temporarily, to alleviate something of his and something of mine, and once again, as I brought his face closer, my hand made certain things vanish and conjured others into existence.

Preventorium. I'd been struck by the word when Wilhelmina had uttered it, an antechamber to disease, she'd said, but surely you could extend it to describe any space where nascent monsters are locked up, crammed on top of each other before they evolve into something more turbulent and harder to control. I thought back on the gallery of situations I'd ended prematurely, a pill for every tension headache when the occasional dose of tension, Wilhelmina would have argued, is necessary in life. At the preventorium you nip things in the bud, disastrous things but also possibly wonderful ones too. You pre-empt it all. And end up with nothing.

Lost child in the gallery, where did you come from and where do you go? What of the beautiful pictures when all you long for is a familiar face? How to retrace your steps when you weren't tracing them to begin with, only following what you thought was a certainty? Have they abandoned you for good, left you there in those long rooms full of laconic faces and unknown landscapes, waiting for someone else to come along and adopt you? People can grasp his distress from afar, this boy who looks up into the face of every adult, confronted with his first taste of eternity. None of the adults in the room, all standing at paintings very serious, seem to own him, and no one echoes his features or colouring. A guard approaches, appears to ask where his parents are. Before he has time to reply, still formulating the answer since he doesn't speak the language of the country, he sees a hand he recognises. He drops his head, sees a familiar pair of shoes. Where have you been? booms a familiar voice. The familiar hand grabs his and pulls him past the paintings and out the door, and there is no longer a lost child in the gallery.

Ever since I'd started at the workshop, every event in life, major, middling or mundane, would be analysed at my buffing machine. An extraction fan dispersed the precious metal dust, or sweep, that'd come wafting out as I polished, and the more dust, the deeper I'd throw myself into my ruminations. That autumn I overshined a great many items.

On Monday I thought about how the whiskey had moved things along, Czech single malt coaxing the story from A to B. And yet with his mother gone, I couldn't help feeling that everything in the home heaved with new life, tentatively at first and then more committedly, the lava lamp releasing its molten interior, spilling thickly under the door of his bedroom. His bedroom. How did we end up there? The whiskey was to blame. But that's where we'd ended, or rather commenced, and my first vision upon waking had been of an imposing map of Holland. THE NETHERLANDS it said in red, white and blue letters that announced themselves into the room. Instead of topographical features the map was dotted with cartoon windmills and clouds, as though the clouds formed a stationary rather than shifting part of the landscape and the windmills were their mountains. From the map I'd turned to look at

Max and was struck by the fact that when awake he seemed lazy and languorous but when asleep he exuded a particular vitality, one arm tight around my waist and a surprisingly muscular leg emerging from under the blanket, eyes closed yet framed by an air of concentration.

Objects I hadn't seen the night before were made visible by the morning light. On the bookshelf near the bed was the lava lamp, regurgitating sunsets. A snow globe with a trapped plastic clown. A stack of board games. An assortment of old cookie tins, and the complete sets of Tintin and Asterix. There was also a photograph of a child sitting on a man's lap, arms and legs thrown out mid-tantrum. This room proposed a shorter time travel than the rest of the home; rather than fling you back to another century it transported you to recent decades. Uncertain what to do with myself, I dressed and began a Tintin. An hour passed. I was thirsty and my temples throbbed. I could go and sit in the living room, open a window and breathe in the air of the canal, but reckoned it might be nicer if I were there when he awoke. I finished the Tintin, began another. It was during the five minutes I left the room, to fetch a glass of water followed by a futile quest for paracetamol, that Max got up. When I returned he was on the edge of the bed slipping on his trousers. Are you hungry, he asked, or just tea? Just tea, I replied, I'm too hungover to eat. Yeah me too, just tea and meds for me and please don't show me anything amber, he said, and after this very brief exchange, within which a less defined plan of action was concealed, I watched as he mashed six cardamom pods, something an Afghan friend once taught him, into a teapot and then added two tea bags and boiling water. He served me that, and the paracetamol I'd requested, and we walked to the living room with our mugs. *Flora Blau*, he said as we nestled into the sofa. I realised last night that if we were to marry your name would become Flora Blau. Almost like Blue Flower. Flora Blau, he said again, a little adventurously, and seemed amused by the thought.

He preferred the hand-painted slides, things like astronomical diagrams, mythological landscapes and archetypal figures that were lovely but lacked dimensionality. I liked the photographic. They had more depth. They were tethered to a particular moment in time and yet they retained an air of mystery: you felt they were hiding something. Hand-painted slides were often round while photographic slides were almost a perfect square, as though corners didn't exist in make-believe worlds and only gritty reality was allowed to reveal its pointy edges. But these geometrical distinctions were only evident when handling the slides outside the lantern, Max reminded me, not when the images were cast. Every now and then we'd come across an index card with handwritten notes in German, a sort of aide-memoire only his mother could have deciphered. A number of slides were cracked, but this added an unintended feature to the scene – a stream, a fissure, a lightning bolt.

Three months after my meeting with Wilhelmina here we were, cross-legged, knees touching, on the rug in her bedroom by the wardrobe. Rather than an intrusion it felt like an assignation. Had Max and I been set up, in the hospital corridor, by someone who suspected she may never be able to do so in person? At moments I wondered whether we'd made a pact, Wilhelmina and I, and I was expected to honour a promise, insinuated rather than explicit. I now understood the hold of the dead raver over the young Belgian, how one brief episode involving a stranger could persist over time.

Max brought out a rectangular cardboard box: the slides she'd taken to Mexico. I held them up one by one, the compressed scenes only feebly evoking their magnified selves, and thought of Wilhelmina at her lantern, the nurses at the door.

Nearly every slide was labelled and had tape around its border. Series were usually accompanied by booklets, supplying narratives to be read aloud. The most cosseted lived in boxes of sturdy wood, their lids lined with green felt. Only these had grooves. In cardboard boxes, slides were pressed together with no separation. And so it was that we held each one up to the lamp and let the light pour through as late afternoon segued into evening and evening into night. Max and I set some aside and returned others to their boxes, and as he blew off the dust and squinted into each glass plate I felt the pull of the past encased in a more immediate longing. Our concentration was shattered by a loud ring. It stopped, then began again. I realised it was my phone, and ran over to my bag by the door.

Can you speak now?

Is something wrong?

Diego is dead.

What?

He's gone.

I made a sign to Max and hurried to the living room and sat down in an armchair, preparing myself. It began that past Sunday, my mother told me. He spent all day in the garden lying on the grass like a sphinx, during which time he didn't sleep or eat or look at them, a vacancy in his eyes she'd seen in dying birds, and he didn't respond to their calls or react when they went over to pet him. It was a struggle to bring him into the house that night, a neighbour had to help, but it'd been out of the question to leave him in the cold. The next morning they drove him to the vet, who said he was running a fever and had to be kept on a drip and under observation. My mother visited daily and after a few days he no longer had a fever and started to eat a little. It was fine for him to return home, the vet said, for his twelfth birthday the following day. So they bundled him into the car and started the journey. But something went terribly wrong, and he died on the way, on a sultry afternoon where even with the windows rolled down the air inside was stuffy and still. With a sudden final yelp, Diogenes died in the Mexico City traffic, an unsettling, unpoetic end. They bought a sack of quicklime and asked the street watchman to dig a grave in the garden by the fig tree.

I'd just hung up with my mother when Max came to find me. I told him I was going home. But we haven't finished. Bad news from Mexico, I said, and left him standing with a slide in his hand. On the bus I thought about my final exchange with Diogenes under the dining-room table. His advanced years, his clouded gaze, his hesitant movements and rickety hind legs. And then further back to when he was a young pup throbbing with muscle and testosterone, to a time when only a few of us had the strength to walk him. I could still feel his thick ruff against my face, the scents of house and garden in his fur. How strange it was that despite these earlier memories my lifelong memento would be the scars on my left hand, scars from one fraught encounter amid thousands of peaceful ones. For the rest of my life, my hand would be marked by his sudden spell of madness.

Outside the house I was surprised to glimpse two figures. My landlords. A rare occurrence, and even more so at half past ten on a Wednesday night. I hadn't seen my landlord since the spider incident and was not in the mood for conversation. I longed to eat something, put a cloth over my burning eyes, and light a candle to Diogenes. But there they were. Their train from the Lake District had encountered severe delays. My landlady looked more tired than ever. Slender with green eyes, she had once been the owner of a fancy yarn shop in Camden Passage. I helped carry her heavy bag up the front steps. Rocks from the seashore, she murmured as she clasped the handrail and took one stair at a time, eyes pinned on the beckoning door. Once inside my landlord reached for his wife's arm, reclaiming her, and one of them said goodnight.

I made myself a sandwich and a cup of mint tea and went to sit by the window. Down below in the garden the faint white of a clothes line threaded the darkness.

No one at work had much inkling what a magic lantern was but they liked the idea of old images thrown in the dark. Things had slowed to a halt over the past few weeks and the mood was turning stagnant, creative thoughts on strike, fantasies adjourned. Kate seemed unlit, Paul longed to depart from the mould. We needed more fire down there, even I had to admit, there wasn't enough to go around all winter or even for the month of November, and when I told them about phantasmagoria, they succumbed. Did I first hear the word from Wilhelmina? *A phantasmagoria of doctors and nurses.* She may have said. Or had I read it in a newsletter? In magic lantern speak it described the ghoulish shows in which monks, nuns and skeletons processioned along the walls of the Capuchin convent in Paris right after the French Revolution, floating out of the lantern onto a white screen or clouds of smoke, many an image lunging towards the spectators as it grew in size since the lantern was on wheels. There'd be the sulphurous smell of candle. Fumes swirling from the lantern's chimney. A whole range of sound effects accompanied the show, including the clanking of chains and the ethereal tones of a glass harmonica. Often Marat and Robespierre were resurrected, and figures from Gothic novels, their faces rippling across the room while revolution roared on the streets overhead.

Unlike other shows, the lantern was hidden from the audience; the phantoms were more real. Some men struck at them with their walking sticks. Smelling salts were at hand for the ladies. The so-called rational mind was still susceptible to illusion. I described the scenario to my colleagues, laying on as much lavish detail as I remembered from the newsletters, and watched the silver glint as Paul turned over a skull in his hand. Whatever ghouls Max chose to project, however outlandish, deviant or displaced, I knew they would be at home in our workshop.

On Fridays Pato would cycle to the British Museum and spend the day sketching. Bizarre things began to happen when he sat for too long in front of objects from antiquity. After a while, he claimed, another energy would break through. He started wearing a black hat with an exceptionally wide rim that would protect him from those forces, he said, as long as he remained under its cover. Whenever he shared his stories I would hide my scepticism, never wanting to hold a pin to his reverie, but even I had been struck by the latest, which like many good stories involved a cat. He'd been sketching in the hall of ancient Egyptian sculpture and was in the midst of drawing Bastet when he felt his hand guided in another direction. No matter how hard he tried to keep to the ancient elegant line, he found himself drawing an ordinary tabby. He showed his curator friend the drawing. Oh, that's Mike. Mike? The coddled feline who lived in the porter's lodge from 1909 to 1929.

This curator, who'd been working at the British Museum for decades and had a hoary landscape of a beard to show for it, produced a booklet dedicated to Mike, and Pato's eager mind absorbed most of the details. First, he told me about the cat's father, Black Jack, by all accounts an arresting creature, black with white paws and chest and formidable whiskers, who loved perching on desks in the old Reading Room and would ask readers to hold the doors open for him when he wanted to exit. One day Black Jack appeared with a scrap of fur in his mouth and deposited it at the feet of Sir Ernest Wallis Budge, the Keeper of Egyptian Antiquities, because of his affinity for the mummies of Egyptian cats. They named the kitten Mike, a curious name for a cat who really should have been called Otto or Horus, but anyway, throughout his life Mike continued to favour the Egyptian section and would prowl its halls at night. During the day he'd stare down pigeons in the colonnade and warily eye the assortment of humanity queuing to enter the museum. And if he saw a dog he would puff out and defend his territory. The waitresses from the refreshment room were said to bring him leftover milk and scraps in the evening. Even during the war, he never went hungry. The museum gatekeepers treated him 'as man and brother', yet Mike's best friend remained Sir Ernest Budge, and he was said to make 'a great fuss' whenever he appeared. After Budge retired he came by every week to contribute sixpence to his larder. By the end of his life, Mike had left an indentation on the shelf in the porter's lodge.

Pato showed me his drawing of this tabby that'd harnessed itself to the cats of ancient Egypt. I had to admit, it did look drawn by another, and as I watched him tape it to the wall of his studio I couldn't help wishing I would someday re-encounter, at a moment when I least expected it, an encore of my dog.

The girls in the shop liked to dress up and add a bit of theatre and presentation, after all, they were our public face and we the more hidden one, the bass section to their clarinet. Sometimes Kate would replicate their smoky eye make-up and fishnet stockings and bring the theatre and presentation below. On the evening of the lantern show her stockings were torn for effect, ladders ascending from the depths of her boots into the heights of her miniskirt.

Two beige moths, surprised by the emergence of light, had fluttered out when I'd extracted the policeman's cape from my cupboard. It was now draped over Max's shoulders. He'd arrived early to set up the lantern on a table two metres from the wall and lay out the slides in the order he would cast them. My visit cut short by the phone call, I had yet to see the images he'd chosen, but he'd been dithering till the end. A little superstition wasn't such a bad thing, he'd said, it keeps our behaviour in check. But collective superstition is a whole other matter. Wilhelmina would bear this in mind when casting old images into the present. He had no idea what would happen if he went near her slides. Look how things got out of hand with her whiskey. What exactly got out of hand? I'd asked. He ignored the question. It will be fine, I reassured him while silently recalling a note I'd seen in one of the newsletters; the editor asked for restoration tips, advice sought for unusual acquisitions, and sightings of magic lanterns in recent films or television, but what interested him the most was to hear about personal experiences of shows given by society members, the more disastrous the better.

The audience would be me, Kate, Paul, Pato, part-time Nick, my friends Lulu and Sadie, and a guitarist who had come into the shop that day looking to replace a pendant he'd lost on tour. He was joined by his sound engineer, a similarly angular fellow. I introduced Pato to everyone and added that his name meant duck in Spanish. Drake, he insisted. Preoccupied with more immediate concerns, Max seemed unfazed by his presence. Only once someone turned off the overhead light did Paul crawl out of the cave at the back. A bit of resistance, I sensed, to a newcomer invading his kingdom. Tools at rest and armed with different levels of expectation, we now sat fanned out across the room. Wouldn't you like some music for your show? asked Kate. Do you have any gamelan? What's that? she said but didn't wait for an answer. A tune by Black Sabbath, now the jeweller, hammered and bludgeoned the room. Max looked mortified. I went over and switched it off.

And then in an instant the first image burst forth in the darkness, its black background suggestive of a funerary announcement, and yet this image quivered with life as it was cast across the room, from tabletop to wall, tin box to smooth plaster, seventeenth-century technology erupting into twenty-first-century space as an old vision bypassed the eras. At first it didn't matter which image it was that emerged from the lantern, most modern gadgetry vexed us to the point of despair, and it was captivating and entrancing and even transgressive to hand ourselves over to something less complicated and possibly more innocent in intention, and we sat back to watch pictures travel from source to site, few of us aware of the intricacies of illusion.

Max opened with the *Catastrophe Series* by York & Sons. Six pairs of hand-coloured slides marked A and B. Tranquil scenes hijacked by disastrous yet often humorous sequels.

> Slide A: an elephant sits at the base of a tree, a monkey perched on the tip of its trunk, teasing it.
> Slide B: the elephant releases a geyser of water, tossing the startled monkey into the air.

> Slide A: a man in a blue waistcoat and striped trousers is being helped onto a mule by his servant.
> Slide B: the mule revolts, bites the man's wrist and kicks the servant.

> Slide A: a man with the face of a glutton sits down to eat a Christmas pudding.
> Slide B: the Christmas pudding morphs into a monstrous head on legs, its arms a knife and fork, and lunges towards the diner, grabs him by the waist, and sends his knife flying.

How quickly, they seemed to be saying, a setting can darken. Max was rigid at the lantern, lacked his mother's flow. The pairs of slides were meant to be in quick succession to best illustrate a before and after, but he was too slow and the comical moments lost their charge.

The dagger-clutching nun, her wailing mouth a gash of red.

The interior of a grotto, with vacant boat and stalactites.

A dancing skeleton. (Blurry at first; he fiddled with the lens until ribs and grimace came into focus.)

Paul rose from his chair and intercepted the beam of light, his face now illuminated a sickly yellow, and for a moment man and ghoul were one. He made a duck with his hands, as though needing to puncture the solemnity, then returned to his seat.

The head of Medusa, upside down.

Max cast Medusa right side up, and then the nun again. Removed her, cast the grotto a second time too.

A ship tilting dangerously in choppy waters a midnight blue.

The head of the Great Sphinx, the sun setting behind her haunches.

He moved on from painted slides to photographic, from colour to black and white. I had the sense the next photographs were all taken by the same person, by someone with a strong interest in rural life who wanted to document it for posterity. They may have been mises en scène of common people in the countryside yet they felt more spectral than any of the painted ghouls.

An old bearded man in a woman's hat, a pipe in his mouth at forty-five degrees. He is knitting a mitten, completely absorbed in the task at hand, as he sits on a fence at the base of a windmill. A ball of yarn in his lap, jacket draped loosely over his shoulders, a worn umbrella propped against his thigh. Two ribbons dangle from his arm. A living cupboard of a man.

Three figures in a graveyard. A blonde girl in braids waters the vegetation with a spouted can. A little boy in an oversized suit watches on. Nearby stands a woman in black, their mother, presumably, beside a tombstone engraved with the name Gustav Rosenbacher. The ivy around the mourners has grown very high, obscuring their lower bodies. You sense they've been gathered there ever since this Gustav passed away yet the ivy, more vibrant than any of the human figures, will never fill the vacancy.

A barefoot man sitting by the side of the road, a dog sprawled out on the grass beside him. His cart also rests nearby, a lopsided vehicle containing heaps of rags, brooms and baskets: stray dogs of cloth and wicker.

Two men with hats and moustaches, carrying baskets of stacked dishes like precarious accordions.

A sequence of more abstract images, also photographic. Their abstraction should have freed things up but they deepened the unease that'd begun with the country folk, a collective sense of loss curdling into something fiercer, and I experienced none of the lightness of Wilhelmina's show, only heaviness, a heaviness so great I couldn't enter the illusion but I also couldn't depart.

A pair of eyes with long lashes at the bottom of a glass of water.

The glass without eyes, perhaps they've dissolved.

The shadow of a man with a wooden leg.

The shadow of his leg joins him.

A small hut.

A row of oak trees.

A path into the forest.

Again, the shadow of a man with a wooden leg.

And finally, almost as an afterthought, Carlota, her figure even more solitary in the depths of our workshop.

Max removed the slide, leaving behind an empty glowing circle. By the time the lights came on he'd tossed the cape he'd been wearing onto a chair, distancing himself from the person who had just performed, and quickly wrapped the lantern in a towel and stuffed the slides this way and that into their boxes. I thought of going over to help but stayed where I was. The others were barely emerging from the spell. There they'd sat, a disparate bunch caught up in a remarkable moment, a moment that took a few seconds to wane. Eventually the musician rose from his chair and said he and the sound engineer were due back at the studio. Paul cleared his throat, as though preparing to speak, but didn't. Kate remained with her legs crossed, hands in lap. I couldn't tell whether she was transfixed by Max, the lantern or the situation. Pato began to clap, softly at first and then more loudly. Lulu and Sadie joined in. But it was too late for any gestures of appreciation. Max had finished and was now at the stairs, his eyes fixed on the *pez diablo* hanging on the wall.

There was no Wilhelmina in the slides, or anywhere. *Aquí se acaba.*

I tried the buzzer a few times, short presses and longer ones, and after waiting a minute or two I gave the door a push, surprised to see it yield. I entered the home and, though no one was watching, removed my shoes. In the living room a sleepiness lay over everything like heavy velvet from a vintage shop. Even the mouse wheel lay silent. I threw open the curtains, unlatched a window, let in the sounds of the canal. From where I stood I could see the magic lantern had been returned to the shelf. A radiance unusual for winter was streaming in and by some wondrous act of refraction a ray of light hit the shoulder of the lantern at just the right angle, sending its silvery essence into the room, and that moment when a sliver of light from outside met with the optical instrument sitting on the shelf not expecting attention felt more mysterious than anything I'd seen activated by a human.

Max entered silently and abruptly as though projected. Nine days had passed since the show. His face was paler, gaunter, clammy. He walked over to the window and closed it. As was his custom he didn't seem surprised to see me or, if he was, he hid it. Tea or beer? he asked instead of a greeting. One of each, please, but there's no hurry. Why don't you sit down for a moment? It's fine, I'll stand. So we stood. I said I'd come to check in. Had he seen my messages? Everyone loved the show. Yes, you wrote that. People are still talking about it. I'm sure they are. I assured him again how much everyone had loved it, my friend Pato was even painting the archer and brooding monk arm-wrestling in a medieval tavern, and Paul was talking about making a ring inspired by something he'd seen although he was keeping it secret for now. And Kate, well, I actually didn't pass on Kate's reaction since she'd asked after him so many times that past week it'd made my hair stand on end. In any case, Max wasn't having it. He went to the kitchen to fetch the drinks.

I walked over to greet the mouse. Isidore was busy grooming himself, one leg raised diagonally as he licked his front toes, nibbling on them one by one. A hill of wood shavings rose beside him, the recent shell of a nap. Upon seeing me he lowered his leg and shifted into a more attentive position. I leaned over and gazed through the lid's wire mesh. A pair of bold sparkly eyes met mine. Perhaps he wanted a caress. I'd seen Max pet him before. He was shy, yes, but he seemed to trust humans. I carefully pushed aside the lid and slid in my right arm. He sniffed my hand, retreated, returned to investigate further. His snout twitched a little, his whiskers quivered. His slender pink tail was almost the length of his body. I gently stroked his head. The fur was soft and thick. I ran my finger from his head down his back. He seemed to be enjoying the contact. I'd never stroked a mouse before and kept expecting him to purr. But instead he pinned back his ears and bit me, a sharp pinch, executed with miniature incisors. I quickly withdrew my hand. The mouse's mouth remained clamped to the tip of my index finger. Without another thought I began waving it wildly this way and that, trying to shake him off. The animal held on for dear life. And before I knew it I'd sent him flying across the room, where he hit an empty patch of wall and went still upon impact. Damn. Damn. Damn. I ran over to pick him up. In my hand he felt like one of the cloth mice the cats at home would play with. I placed his limp body back in the tank moments before Max returned to the room with the tea and beer on a round tray.

How to explain what had just happened, an instant that had spooled out of control, a reaction, an overreaction, to a small but sudden assault, although the mouse had acted in self-defence. Max went over to the stereo and put on some music. The notes of a synth sprang into the room, electronic notes joined by a young voice lost in a forest, with the tune of a hurdy-gurdy layered in.

The mouse would hear none of it.

Max handed me my drinks. I've been thinking about getting back into music, he said, and just found this tape of my old band. Wolf Spider in the Nursery. *Had there been such a spider?* Yes, he said, but not in the nursery. I drank the beer, sipped the tea, aimed to listen. Every now and then voice and beats would find one another and produce something almost noble but just as that noble encounter was unfolding the voice would decide to go down another path and wreck the marriage. I told Max the story of the dead raver, dead in a sea of techno, and how the DJ had brought the night to a halt, demanding a minute of silence, though what I really wanted to say, of course, what I really wanted to request, was a minute of silence for the dead mouse. But I carried on as if nothing had happened.

He fussed at the stereo, adjusting tone, treble and bass. Each time I would glance over at the tank. The glass walls displayed no signs of movement. And then I'd quickly glance down at my finger, the skin only lightly broken, a thin red line below the nail, the fingertip a bit swollen. A mouse bite was probably at the very low end of the bite-force chart, surely worlds away from a dog bite, although I now remembered reading about the grinding teeth of the Mexican volcano mouse in a *National Geographic*. The more minutes that passed, the harder to tell him. And his peculiar behaviour complicated things further. He seemed equally tired and wired, listless one moment, jittery the next. I searched for a box of plasters in the bathroom cabinet. *Measure the wound to use the right size plaster*, but the plasters only came in two sizes, neither quite small nor wide enough for a mouse bite. I chose two of the smaller ones and wrapped them around my finger.

Do you have any more of that whiskey? Half a bottle, he said. Toasting to the wolf spider and its electronic emissions, we knocked back a shot, and another and another until Max held the bottle upside down and shook out the last drops. I'd hardly returned my glass to the table when he threw himself onto me. I did not push him away, nor did I welcome his advances, and as he buried his face in my neck all I could think about was the mouse who, up until an hour or two ago, had been carrying on with his creaturely rhythms. What had happened to my relationship to the animal kingdom? We had always been on exceptional terms, the animal kingdom and I, apart from the occasional mosquito I never killed anything and hadn't eaten an animal since I was twelve, but there'd been a recent shift and I failed to understand why. If these animal bites were karmic returns then what exactly was I paying for, what sort of retribution was being demanded of me from some four-footed god? Even the cats at home would probably now avoid me and stop coming up to my rooms, a warning issued to all other species. To other species, that is, except the human. Max seemed entirely unaware of my indisposition. We were now in his room and all of his weight was on me. I put my hands on his shoulders and pushed him aside. It was easier than expected. Once beside me, he drifted off into a drunken sleep. He would not be sleeping this peacefully if he knew. I should have told him. But there was no hurry.

In the glow of the lava lamp I could see the imposing map of the Netherlands. At moments it seemed like the map was breathing, its breaths matching Max's, the paper lifting off the wall each time he exhaled. Perhaps he was there now, wandering about the canals or holding up a shield to the wind. I tried to sleep but couldn't shut out the map. In the early hours, unable to bear the situation any longer, I shook him awake. The mouse is dead, I told him. What are you talking about? The mouse. Go and see for yourself, I said, the tension returning to his body as he leapt out of bed, almost stumbling, and ran out. I couldn't bring myself to follow. Before long he would be back in a mess. At that very moment he was probably crumpling in front of the tank or weeping into a cushion or clenching his fists. Minutes later he returned. Instead of anguish he wore a smile, and in his left hand cradled Isidore. The mouse lifted his head and looked around, his bright eyes taking in the unexplored territory of the bedroom. All good, Max said, all good.

My ledger of Britain contained many empty pages, a great swathe I had yet to explore, but I had never liked boats. I hated the sensation of being rocked, hated feeling captive offshore. Someone had slipped an envelope under Max's front door containing two tickets for a paddle steamer down the Thames. Courtesy of Grietje De Vries, a Dutch family friend. The last seagoing paddle steamer of its kind. Destination: Gravesend. The name had reminded her of 's-Gravenhage, for which Den Haag, The Hague, was an abbreviation. And even more of Willem Jacob 's Gravesande, the Dutch mathematician and philosopher and early populariser of the magic lantern. Yet it had nothing to do with either. Would I come along? Gravesend, Max spoke into the phone with more emphasis. One of the last towns before England opens up to the North Sea. And where *Heart of Darkness* begins. I'd heard of the book, yes. He uttered the name yet again, as though it should have sparked countless associations in my mind. He told me to look at a map on my phone. It appeared as nothing more than an insignificant point right after a twist in the Thames. And still didn't mean anything to me. But before hanging up he added a few words that sealed it. We would use the occasion, he said, to scatter Wilhelmina's ashes.

The night before our trip, I had a dream. Max,

Wilhelmina and I are standing on the canal path. The sky is streaked purple and green. It's hard to tell the time of day. As we stand there great wooden toys in the shapes of animals start floating past, one by one. Lemur. Goose. Pangolin. Lion. Chanting fills the air as a long narrow boat, more boat-shaped than the others, sails towards us. It is full of children. These are the Children of the Boat, Wilhelmina says. Their chanting grows louder. *Diogenes is dead, Diogenes is dead.* As they approach I notice that the children are old and have carved wooden faces. Wilhelmina says they are hungry. She and Max start throwing rolls at them but the rolls land in the water and float. *Diogenes is dead*, the children continue to chant. To Max's and Wilhelmina's ears their words are cries of hunger. The rolls do not reach the children. Slowly the boat sails off and the chanting fades. All I hear now is the rippling current in my ear. I awoke to find one of the cats lapping at the glass of water by my bed.

Item 72-0627

For donation

TWELVE BOXES OF MAGIC LANTERN SLIDES

Some cracked, no full sets, just odds and ends.
Don't want anything for them. But they would need to be collected.
I live in London, England.

The cold nipped at my face as I headed towards Tower Bridge that Sunday morning, the weak sun reflecting off the tall mirrored buildings, and met Max at the pier. The boat was waiting, a giant toy attached to a thick rope, and we joined the slow queue of pensioners as they gripped the side rails. We appeared to be the only passengers under seventy. It reminded him of Scheveningen. Once on deck an elderly couple, perhaps noticing my companion's sullen expression, made room for us on a bench. The horn blew, followed by the captain's announcement on the loudspeaker. Brawny figures untethered the boat from the dock. We pulled away from the shore and began our journey down the Thames, our bench close enough to the edge to feel the river's spray. Max commented on the perilous position of the smokestacks, tilting at an angle overhead, and I tried to reassure him that whatever helps a ship maintain an even keel most likely doesn't produce the same stability in people.

Flora? a voice, not Max's, uttered nearby.

It took me a moment to recognise my landlords, in their toggle coats and knitted hats. I had no choice but to introduce both parties, and as they eyed Max I could almost see thought bubbles forming above their heads – who was this character and had he ever been in their home? – and after an awkward exchange about the darkening skies despite a promising forecast my landlords headed into the sheltered area of the vessel, but not before returning our worries to the table. So you're going all the way to Gravesend, my landlord had said. Well, we're getting off before that. Don't you know the worst ever disaster on an inland waterway in this country is associated with Gravesend? No, we didn't. They would spare us the details. And anyway, things were much safer now. They wished us a good journey.

Once the final bridge of London had been left behind we steamed past old warehouses, balconied residential buildings and glimmering towers of commerce, past Canary Wharf, Surrey Quays and Greenwich, the water turning rougher before it opened up. Yet for those two hours and fifteen minutes I focused above all on the face in front of me. Exposed to the morning light, beyond the corners and shadows of his home. Though we'd met outdoors before, how else to put it but that today he looked oxidised. Was this the destiny, I had to ask myself, of everything that sees daylight? I continued to study the landscape that was again on the verge of losing its appeal. Puckish ears and pale eyes, indecisive in colour. Blue but not blue. Pasty skin. Clammy. Short curls brushed to the side, protesting. The only feature he shared with his mother was the brow, though most of the time his was covered, apart from when a gust of wind parted the hair at the front. At moments I sensed him studying me with similar ambivalence.

A drizzle set in. Umbrellas sprang open. We hadn't brought one. Huddled on the bench like pigeons under an inhospitable sky, I had the sensation we, or at least our emotions, were ageing as we steamed onwards and that by the time we reached Gravesend we would have caught up with our fellow passengers. Halfway through the journey, long after the warehouses had surrendered to a flat expanse of water, we descended a flight of stairs to the engine room to admire the machinery, beautiful pipes and pistons, their movement upwards, downwards and sideways. This engine was our ferryman conducting us down the causeway, its mechanical loops so hypnotic we could have remained there for the rest of the journey, but the loud clanking sent us back to the blustery deck.

Historically Gravesend was where coastal pilots ceded to riverine, yet I sensed no shift in mood, only a shrinking of vistas, once we arrived. Hands in pockets and coats fully buttoned, we started our trudge through the streets, past endless TO LET signs and desolate caffs, pausing every now and then to inspect a building's weary face or an abandoned shopfront exhibiting the precarious fate of many a seaside town. I'd visited coastal towns in the past, melancholy places with crumbling pavilions selling sweets and promises from other times, but this one took coastal depression to another level and under the drizzle we tramped its silent streets, into dead ends and neglected alleyways, every now and then coming across a hesitant voice of gentrification in the form of a tiny art house or gallery space. For the most part, however, the town exuded an off-season air, as though we'd chosen the worst possible day in the calendar to visit. The damp, the gusts, the desolation: it all got under my coat.

How about lunch? I suggested.

The Three Daws was an old mariners' pub on the riverbank, its outer walls splashed by countless tides, its inner walls bristling with legends of smugglings and hauntings as well as portraits of Pocahontas, who upon falling ill had disembarked at Gravesend with her husband John Rolfe and died on its shores. We found a table in the corner and ordered pints and jacket potatoes. My landlord's words still ringing in his head, Max pulled out his phone and looked up the disaster associated with Gravesend. Sometime in the late 1870s a paddle steamer was returning to London from a 'moonlight trip' to the Kent coast when it collided with a collier. The captain had replaced his helmsman at Gravesend for a man with limited knowledge of the river. Most of the passengers who drowned lost their lives in filthy water since the ship split in two and sank at the very spot of London's sewage pumping stations at Barking. One hour before the collision, millions of gallons of raw sewage had been released into the river. Around 650 passengers died, including many children. A large number of passengers couldn't swim and even those who could were weighed down by their heavy Victorian clothes.

Reminding him of our mission, I nodded towards the bag of ashes on the empty chair between us, but that only fed his agitation. He still tortured himself for not flying out. She had told him to stay put. Stay put, she'd said, it will only make matters worse if you come. He should have gone anyway. It might have made a difference. It might not have. He would never know. There were so many things he would like to know. He pushed away his plate, edging it to the far end of the table until it could go no further.

And then Holland returned, with the image of Dutch women at their windows, rags in hand, and I realised it was these women who were always polishing a pane to the past, and from these industrious women he travelled to the windy treacherous beach of his childhood and from there to Intlekoffer, and as he sat very still, decanting his memories, I couldn't help sensing he wanted to pass them on, all these faces that had accumulated over the years, some in soft focus and others more distinct. He told me about their last visit, eight years after Jan died. First stop, the Mauritshuis, where Wilhelmina had roamed the rooms impatiently, pausing in front of a still life featuring a stack of cheeses, and then in front of a still life featuring several loaves of bread, then one with clusters of green and purple grapes. Very soon her appetite surpassed any need for culture. Second stop, a cafe where they ordered a mountain of *poffertjes* under a snowstorm of powdered sugar. Third stop, Intlekoffer. Max protested. But his mother wanted to go back. By then everyone had aged a decade and in that decade the antiquarian too had lost his spouse. His hair had turned a frozen canal white, his knees had given up, and his hand had developed a tremor. But he continued to postpone the day he would close his shop. His entire life, or at least all of the important moments, had unfolded in that space. He remained faithful to the past in other ways, too. Hanging near the till was an Indonesian puppet Wilhelmina had set aside nine years earlier, on the day she'd purchased the lantern. Attached to its foot was a tag with her name. Every once in a while a customer had enquired into it, but would be told it wasn't for sale. After offering them tea and *speculaas*, Intlekoffer took them to a room at the back of the shop occupied by toys he'd either made or nursed back to life with such dedication he felt like their maker. And in that tiny room, surrounded by cloth puppets and mannequins, his diminishing faith became palpable. The solitude of the old toymaker. Widowed and bereft, this old man spoke to them of how every night he would wander the icy, inanimate streets of The Hague and upon returning home from his walks he would look at the toys and tell himself that these objects were nothing more than a coloured material dream. And in the inertia of objects the old toymaker confronted his own solitude, which bit more deeply than ever. After that visit, Wilhelmina hardly spoke for days.

Take the lantern, Flora, he said. As long as you keep it and don't sell it on. I may want it back someday. You can have some of the slides too. I didn't answer immediately. Did I want it in my home, this old instrument that might always unsettle? But we had crossed the ocean together, the lantern and I, and the more I'd known about its maker and Wilhelmina's attachment, the greater the affinity. I accepted and thanked him, though I knew I was doing him a favour too.

Outside the pub it took a moment to steady ourselves, the beer having thrown things off-kilter, and we ended up taking a winding route to the port, past more shuttered shops and people. Max pointed out the procession of merchants on the high street and told me their order could be read as a narrative of the place: an ALDI followed by a pound shop followed by a Czech, Polish, Hungarian shop called Monika's International followed by a closed barber shop and a mobile phone shop, all ending with a butcher's Union Jack in the window. But who was to say when we were both partly from here and partly from elsewhere, and as we walked past the shops I felt as foreign as when I'd first arrived as a student.

On our way down to the port we swerved left into an unpaved road and walked until we could walk no further, and there we stopped in front of a grand dilapidated house. It was the last in the row. Max lit a cigarette, took a few drags, passed it to me. The house was remarkably narrow, and its facade a montage of different paints, each layer parting ways with the one beneath. The splintered door had two bells and a crooked mail slot. Through the broken windows I could see the shoulder of a wardrobe and other pieces of furniture expressing reserve. Max too seemed drawn to the house, and as we passed the cigarette back and forth till the filter grew soggy I had a vision of each of us giving up our homes and moving here to Gravesend and renovating this ruin that hadn't received any upkeep in who knew how long, this crumbling structure could be salvaged only in the maddest and most steely of pursuits, Max would fix the roof and I would replace the windows and repaint the door. We would add a few flowerpots and remove the broken glass and the stack of old saucepans by the entrance and it would be so very satisfying, wouldn't it, to observe a work in progress and see it evolve over time.

Upon arriving in Gravesend we'd declared: a bag of ashes, a few handfuls of expectation, £35.76 in my wallet and 'max £25' in his, a full pack of Lucky Strikes purchased that morning from a newsagent's in Tower Bridge, a lighter, two phones, a pen.

Upon leaving we'd declared: a bag of ashes, exhaustion, a half-met hunger for unspecified things, £7.45 in my wallet (lunch was on me) and around £9.50 in his, a lighter, two phones, a pen, and 1/5 of a pack of Lucky Strikes.

The paddle steamer ploughed past the Thames Barrier just as the sun had started its descent and central London rose into view. I'd taken little notice of this construction on our way over but the odd cylinders now called to mind a beautiful scratched slide of four boulders in the sea with gulls gliding over waves of turquoise.

It was just as we'd gone past this barrier that he motioned

to me that the time had come. The vessel was significantly emptier than on the way to Gravesend, many of the passengers would have booked one way and gone home on the train, and we headed towards the deserted stern. He cast the first handful into the air. The ash sifted down onto the water and floated like a pale dismembered flower. I followed his example and plunged my hand into the bag, the contents of which felt like coarse, gritty sand, and scattered another fistful to the wind. The ash blew upwards on a current while other bits remained suspended mid-air, and some flew into my eyes, and as I wiped my eyes I noticed a tiny clump that pirouetted in place as our boat ploughed onwards, and we took turns releasing handful after handful of Wilhelmina, the ash ever more powdery between our fingers, and once we had reached the bottom of the bag Max folded it up and put it in his pocket. I went to sit on a bench. He remained by the railing and took a few steps closer to the edge. I called out his name. He didn't turn. I called again. No response. I went over and drew him away from where he stood. Come sit, I said. What for? For this, I found myself saying, and pointed to him and me and the space in between. I then looked down at the waves, down into the paddle steamer's frothy impetuous wake, and as Max put his arms around me, tentative at first and then with more confidence, I saw a face come into focus and then swiftly dissolve across the surface of the water.

An empty glass slide.

No image, only fingerprints.

Accidental design, the capture of a moment, impossible to recreate.

Acknowledgements

There are many friends who greatly enhance my life but I shall limit myself to those who in some way or other contributed to the existence of this book: first and foremost, magic lanternists Jeremy and Carolyn Brooker, for a marvellous collaboration. Mathilde Bonnefoy, Devorah Baum, Lorna Scott Fox, Simon Schama. Also Josh Appignanesi, Pato Bosich, Michael Bucknell, Clare Carolin, Pablo Calva, Erica Davies of the Ragged School Museum, Sonali Deraniyagala, Maria Dimitrova, Andrew Durbin, Gareth Evans, Iain Forsyth and Jane Pollard, Jasper Gibson, Anouchka Grose, Paul Heber-Percy, Jennifer Higgie, Stewart Home, Mary Horlock, Juliet Jacques, Andrew Kidd, Helga von Kügelgen, Helder Macedo, Tom McCarthy, Simon Moretti, Helen Oyeyemi, Dalila Pasotti, Gerard Passannante, Fiona Shaw, Guy Stagg, Francesca Wade. And everyone at the Swedenborg Society. Thank you to my wonderful agent Tracy Bohan, and Ben Oldfield, as well as Kaiya Shang and Clara Farmer, my editors at Chatto, and managing editor Rhiannon Roy, for their patience with my endless tinkering. For the book's future life in the U.S., I thank Chris Kraus and Semiotext(e).

And for their support: Fondo Nacional para la Cultura y las Artes and Arts Council UK.

The epigraph is from Thomas Creech's 1682 translation of Lucretius's *De rerum natura,* which surely deserves a larger readership. I'm also grateful to the following sources: Stephen Greenblatt's *The Swerve: How the Renaissance Began* and the British Museum's 1929 pamphlet on Mike the museum cat, and newsletters from the Magic Lantern Society.

This novel is dedicated to my beloved parents, and Eva and Josephine.

About the Author

Chloe Aridjis is the author of *Book of Clouds*, which won the Prix du premier roman étranger in France, *Asunder* and *Sea Monsters*, winner of the PEN/Faulkner Award for Fiction. She writes for various art journals and was a guest curator at Tate Liverpool. In 2014 she was awarded a Guggenheim Fellowship. Her most recent book is the collection *Dialogue with a Somnambulist: Stories, Essays and a Portrait Gallery*. She lives in London.